# WILLIE'S REDNECK TIME MACHINE

## JOHN LUKE ROBERTSON

### WITH TRAVIS THRASHER

TYNDALE HOUSE PUBLISHERS, INC., CAROL STREAM, ILLINOIS

**Library of Congress Cataloging-in-Publication Data**

Robertson, John Luke.
  Willie's redneck time machine / John Luke Robertson ; with Travis Thrasher.
    pages cm. — ([Be your own Duck Commander ; #1])
  ISBN 978-1-4143-9813-6 (sc)
  I. Thrasher, Travis, 1971- II. Title.
  PZ7.R5465Wil 2014
  [Fic]—dc23                                      2014016931

Printed in the United States of America

20   19   18   17   16   15   14

7    6    5    4    3    2    1

*This book is dedicated to my dad, Willie.*
*Dad, you've taught me how to laugh at myself,*
*how to love others, and how to keep my faith strong.*
*There's never a dull moment when you're around,*
*and I'm proud to be your son.*

# WARNING!

## DON'T READ THIS BOOK STRAIGHT THROUGH!

You'll miss out on all the fun if you do.

Instead, start at the beginning and decide where to go at the end of each chapter. Follow the instructions on which page number to go to once you make your decision. You'll be flipping around a lot, but that's part of the journey.

When you're done with one story, start over again at the beginning of the book. There are lots of stories packed into this book and lots of different endings.

The great thing is, *you* are the main character. *You* make the decisions.

And right now, *you* get to be the Duck Commander.

Just make sure you don't get shot or bitten or stuck back in 1990. (You can't actually die during time travel, though. If something really bad happens, you'll still be okay.)

We only want the journeys to turn out fun.

Oh, and also, avoid the heavy rains. You *really* don't want to get caught in those.

# THIS IS WHO YOU ARE

**BEFORE WE BEGIN, THIS IS WHO YOU ARE.**

Your name is Willie Jess Robertson.

You are the president of Duck Commander and Buck Commander. You make duck calls and decoys—stuff every good hunter needs.

Your parents are Phil and Kay Robertson. Phil likes to hunt and Miss Kay likes to cook.

You have three brothers: Alan, Jase, and Jep. And a funny ole uncle named Si.

You have a beard, and you're the most handsome of all the Robertson boys. You're the smartest, too, which is why you are the CEO, obviously. Running Duck Commander and Buck Commander keeps you pretty busy, but you know what they say: "Work hard, play hard."

Your wife's name is Korie. She's smart and beautiful and the rock of your life.

You have five kids: John Luke, Sadie, Rebecca, Will, and Bella.

You're also a part-time secret agent, but nobody knows about that, so let's not tell anyone. That's for another story.

You don't know it, but you're about to embark on a crazy awesome adventure.

So rub your beard for luck. Or rub your imaginary beard. Okay, you're ready.

# TODAY

AN ORDER FOR TEN THOUSAND duck calls just got phoned in, and not a single soul is here to be found.

The Duck Commander warehouse is empty. Everybody's at lunch.

This is a problem, but only you seem to mind.

You're waiting on John Luke to show up so you can go shopping with him. It's Korie's birthday party tonight, and the two of you still need to get her presents.

Look, it's not your fault she didn't tell you what to get her. She said she didn't need anything, but you know for a fact if you don't get her anything, you're totally in trouble.

Last time she "didn't need anything," you didn't get her anything. That didn't go over so well.

The problem is, there's this large order for Triple Threat

duck calls, and it looks like you have only ten left in the warehouse. You told Jase and Si, but they nodded and then went out to find some burgers.

You're trying to run a business, and they're trying to find burgers.

You also need to figure out a birthday present. As you walk through the warehouse, you try to come up with ideas. Your ideas are usually pretty amazing.

*Maybe she'd like some kind of nice jewelry.*

The ladies love the sparkly stuff.

*Maybe a getaway trip with the girls.*

You think about this, then change your mind.

*How about a getaway trip for the two of us?*

'Cause that means you'll be able to go somewhere fun too.

Yeah, that's a good idea. Or maybe stick with some chocolates. Like several boxes' worth of them. Or what about one of those giant teddy bears they show on TV? Nah, maybe not.

You find a box of miscellaneous junk and pick out a two-foot dagger in a sheath. This is from a church play you guys put on around Thanksgiving. You take the blade out of its leather holder. It's very real and very sharp. Maybe it would make a very awesome present.

*That's a very dumb idea.*

All of a sudden, you hear Britney Spears singing in your

pocket. Your cell phone is going off, and the song "Oops! . . . I Did It Again" is set as the ringtone. Someone played a trick on you, changing your ringtone, and you haven't been able to change it back yet. You don't recognize the number, so you ignore the call, then make a mental note that you need to fix the ringtone ASAP. Or get John Luke to.

You're almost back to your office when you see something you've never witnessed before. Something that's *seriously* out of place.

It's a wooden outhouse—rectangular with faded old wood and a roof shaped like an upside-down V. It's like one you'd see in the middle of the woods, the kind Uncle Si and your dad, Phil, told you they used when they were kids—the kind you wouldn't want to enter even if your life and bladder depended on it.

*Except something's different about this outhouse.*

On the roof are two things that look like large bulbs. As if the outhouse has antennas. There's also some kind of control panel on the door.

"What in the world . . . ?" you start to say.

Obviously someone is playing another trick on you.

The outhouse is right in the middle of the warehouse, right where a forklift might be heading at any moment.

Someone has to be pulling your leg.

It's close to Korie's office, so maybe it has something to

do with her birthday. Surely she didn't buy an old outhouse at one of those antique shows she goes to.

You walk up to it and check it out. Yeah, it's real. You tap on its side. The wood is thick and dense and has grooves in it. The door has a hole cut into it, maybe for ventilation. It's in the shape of a duck.

*This is totally a prank.*

You press the control panel right below the opening, but none of the buttons work. It looks a bit like one of those computer games for little kids with about a dozen different buttons and a small screen.

You circle the outhouse and see that it's unlike any you've ever seen. And you've seen a few in your life. It reminds you of a Port-A-Potty, and you've got memories of some of those. Especially some of those Port-A-Poops in the early days, the ones that were falling apart, the kind with horrible smells, the kind that really . . .

Well, yeah, you don't want to think about that.

At least this one doesn't stink.

*Why would anybody use one of these when they could just go outside?*

You're about ready to open the door when you hesitate.

*Wait a minute . . .*

That's exactly what they want you to do.

You look around to see if anybody's spying on you. To

see if there's a camera anywhere. But nobody and nothing can be seen.

"I know this is a prank," you call out. "Very funny, Jase!"

Your voice echoes in the silence.

"Oh, and if you're watching me, go make a thousand Triple Threats while you're at it."

Nobody responds. You stare at the closed door of the wooden outhouse.

So why aren't you opening it?

You picture it filled with something. Water, maybe. Or balloons. No, not balloons—that's not creative enough.

Maybe something like shaving cream.

No, you could get out of the way of that.

Maybe some kind of animal. Yeah, that's what *you'd* do if you pulled the old Port-A-Potty–in–the–warehouse prank on someone.

Maybe it's an opossum or a snake. What if it's a skunk? Surely they wouldn't put a skunk in the warehouse. That would be going too far, even for them. Maybe it's some kind of bird. Or maybe several different animals.

*Bats. I can see Jase getting some bats and putting them in this thing.*

But it's not your birthday. It's Korie's. So why would someone be pranking *you*?

You put your ear close to the door. Not on it, of course—just close enough to hear. But you don't hear anything. There's nothing moving inside. You look into the duck-shaped opening on the door, but you can't make out a thing.

"Dad?"

You turn and see John Luke standing there.

"Are we going?" he asks.

"You know what this is all about?" you ask him.

He shakes his head. As he does, you notice something funny about him.

"Did you change your hair?" you ask.

"Yep. You like it?"

You just stare at him. "You have a mullet."

"Yes, sir."

"Why'd you get a mullet?"

"'Cause I'm gonna bring it back."

"Mullets are never coming back," you tell John Luke. "I had one in high school, and—believe me—they're staying in the past."

John Luke pulls at the long hair sticking out below his ears. You roll your eyes.

"So did Jase put this thing here?"

"I don't know," John Luke says.

You nod. You know when your son's up to something, and right now John Luke doesn't have that look on his face.

"Did you open it?" he asks.

"*I'm* not opening that door."

"Why not?"

"'Cause I think someone's pulling a prank on me. Look at that thing. An outhouse? With antennas? Come on. In the middle of the warehouse?"

"I'll open it," John Luke says, grinning as he starts to tug on the handle.

"Wait a minute," you call out, stopping him.

"What?"

You haven't heard anything. You haven't seen anything. You haven't even *smelled* anything. Which is definitely a plus.

"I think we should wait," you tell your son again.

John Luke waits, then decides to keep opening the door.

He tries the handle, but it won't budge. Then he tries pressing a few of the buttons—some of the same ones you pressed—and the door moves on its own.

"How'd you do that?" you ask.

"Press the red button. The one that says Open."

*Oh.*

As the door swings, you squint, expecting some kind of something to come out.

But nothing is there.

"See, it's empty."

It looks just like . . . an outhouse might look.

There's a bench with a hole in it. It's that simple.

John Luke steps into the structure. "It doesn't look used," he says. "No poop on the seat."

You look back once again to see if someone is watching you. Then you hear the door shut.

You wait a moment for John Luke to come out. But he doesn't.

You wait for another second. But no.

Then something weird happens. Those antenna-like things on top of the outhouse turn red and start to blink. They flash like this for a few seconds, then stop.

Again you wait for John Luke to emerge, but he never does. So you decide to open the door. Button pressed, the door swings wide open on its own.

"Hey, come on. Get out of there."

You look into the same space John Luke stepped into.

It's empty.

*Nobody's* there.

"John Luke," you call out.

You peer into the dark corners but don't see anything. There's no way he could be hiding anywhere inside because it's not big enough.

"Hey, John Luke, where'd you go?"

You circle the outhouse but don't see any sign of him.

*Ah, this must be the prank. Some magic trick.*

Maybe someone hired a magician for Korie's birthday. A magical outhouse. There's something you've never heard of before.

"Okay, pretty funny. I'm impressed."

You get back to the entrance and open the door again. You look inside.

John Luke is nowhere around.

He's totally vanished.

You laugh, knowing someone's watching you. Your brothers are having a good ole time.

"Very funny."

You glance around and wait. But nobody says a word. Nobody comes out of the shadows.

Nothing happens. For one minute. Two minutes.

"Come on, John Luke. Seriously."

Silence.

You sigh and look back at the door.

You gotta do something.

Do you step inside the outhouse to check it out yourself? Turn to page 29.

Do you stay outside and wait to see who's playing a trick on you? Turn to page 63.

# TODAY

**SI IS RIGHT AFTER ALL.**

This *is* a time machine. Or at least it sure looks like it.

If this is still all a setup, well . . . they sure must have found a great set designer to make it look like the control room of a spaceship—or a time machine.

The walls are covered with monitors and buttons, and there's a whole circular control panel in the center of the room you're standing in. You're not sure how everything changed from a tiny little outhouse to this, but you're also not sure about a lot of things.

*Like where did John Luke and Jase and now Si all go?*

A button on the wall closest to you starts blinking, and you feel that it must be pushed. It's marked with the number 2319. . . . Could that mean the year 2319? You don't hesitate—you've hesitated enough.

As soon as you jab the button with a finger, the machine springs into motion. You're beginning to feel a bit queasy in your stomach—could be the elk meat you ate for breakfast—when the machine stops with a shudder and the door pops open. You can hear explosions right outside. It sounds like you've entered some kind of arcade center. Either that or there's a war outside this machine . . . probably a futuristic war if it's the year 2319.

In some weird way, as you make your way to the door, you have this strange sense of déjà vu.

*I've done this before.*

But you really haven't. (Unless, of course, you're a reader and you've gone on several journeys already.) Whether you've been here before or not, though, you're sure you hear bomb blasts and something that sounds more like lasers firing than guns.

Maybe you shouldn't leave the safety of your surroundings until the blasts stop. And it might be a good idea to search the machine for a weapon. That dagger from the warehouse would really come in handy about now. But every time machine should have a super high-powered armory, right?

Do you step out of the machine without looking for a weapon? (Really, do you? Truly, should you?) Go to page 145. But seriously. Come on, man.

Do you explore the machine for something to protect yourself with? Go to 71.

# ????

YOU'RE STUDYING YOUR SURROUNDINGS, as best you can in the dark.

Without warning, the room lights up and a large, red-headed man emerges from somewhere in the back of the mystery outhouse. He's got a thick beard and towers over you.

"Can I help you with something?" he asks.

It takes you a second to recover from his surprise entrance. "Yeah, I have some questions."

"There are lots of inquisitive people like you who need answers to feel better about the journey."

"Who are you?" you ask.

"I know about time."

You study him for a minute. "Are you, like, Father Time?"

He laughs and rubs his beard. "That's silly. Mr. Claus gets the same question everywhere he goes."

"Santa?" you ask. *I've always known there was a real Santa!*

"My name is Raymond," the man says. "What do you need to know?"

You point at the complicated-looking console in front of you. "What is this thing?"

"Allow me." He shows you the control panel and begins to guide you through working it . . . and then he stops.

"It's too confusing. You'll never be able to understand it," he says. "This device is a doorway to other places. You're able to experience these locations and times from long ago or in the future."

"You mean, this really is a time machine?"

Raymond nods.

You can hardly believe it. You have so many questions, you don't even know where to begin.

Raymond keeps going. "Let me make sure you get the most important thing. We want these journeys to be fun. So you can't die in another time or place. There are no tragedies here. There are unexplained events, but no deaths."

This sounds kind of familiar. But you can't help feeling worried. "Why not?"

"Level 34-B bicode."

"Say what?"

"Okay. Take the grandfather paradox, for example. You

can't go back in time to kill your grandfather because that would mean you'd never exist, right?"

"I guess so," you say. "But if I don't die, what happens?"

"You'll find yourself back where you began," Father Time—er, Raymond—says mysteriously. "With a vague memory, perhaps, of what you experienced."

You open your mouth to start asking more questions.

"Why do you need the answers so badly?" he says before you're able to ask anything. "Enjoy the ride. The journey is everything, isn't it?"

*Hmmm.*

**Do you ask Raymond to send you wherever John Luke went? Go to page 59.**


**Do you say good-bye to Raymond, then pull a random lever in the middle of the console? (Really? Is this a smart idea?) Go to page 33.**

# TODAY

**BAD THING YOU PICKED DUCK.**

The ducks get all the credit. The poor bucks don't ever get noticed.

You open the door to find water seeping in. You're in the Dog, which is a part of the bayou—a place where you commonly go duck hunting. The outhouse is bobbing up and down. Somehow it's managing to stay upright without toppling over—obviously there's technology happening here that's a bit beyond your comprehension. But regardless, water is coming in, so all of you have to get out.

"We're going to lose the machine!" you say.

"We're going to drown if we don't get out of here," Jase says. "I don't want my tombstone to say 'died in an outhouse'!"

The three of you manage to get out of the time machine before it fills completely. But now you're in the lake, splashing around.

Several ducks find you and land nearby.

"Wish I had my gun," Jase says.

"Wish you had a brain," you tell him.

"Did you pick Duck or Buck?" John Luke asks.

The ducks quack as if they're mocking all of you.

"What do *you* think?"

"I think you chose *poorly*," John Luke says.

"Korie is so gonna kill us," you tell them.

Then you start swimming, trying to avoid the ducks on your way to shore.

## THE END

# A LONG, LONG TIME AGO

THIS PLACE IS TOTAL DARKNESS. And for a while, you wonder if it really is the ark since you don't hear any animals. But then you turn a corner, and it's as if you suddenly enter a zoo. You realize you started in an unused part of this boat but that this deck has what sounds like hundreds of rooms of animals.

You still can't see a thing, so you only detect the animals by noise or smell. You pass a room that rings with the squawks of a thousand birds. Another room has lots of shuffling going on in it. Then you walk right into an animal that lets out a loud "hee-haw." You pet it and feel its ears, then shake your head.

*I end up on an entire boat full of animals and the first one I run into is a screaming donkey.*

You keep moving, trying to locate any human being.

This boat is so big you think you could end up spending hours lost in the darkness. It's like being inside the biggest indoor mall in the world with all the lights out and no way to get in touch with anybody.

As you silently walk down another darkened hallway, you hear something to your left.

"Willie?"

Your name seems to hover all around you. You recognize Phil's voice but can't see him.

"Come over here. Be quiet."

You enter a room to your left. There you can hear ducks.

"Phil, is that you?" you ask.

You always call your dad by his first name. This dates back to when you started working with Duck Commander and wanted to be professional and grown-up. It's stuck since then.

"I could see you a mile away," he says.

There's a little light coming through a small hole the size of your fist.

"It's a makeshift window," Phil tells you. "I have a piece of wood that fits inside it to keep too much rain from coming in."

"We gotta get out of here."

Phil nods. "You got that right."

"Did you . . . did you want to come back here to Noah's time?"

"Of course I did. I've always wanted to see what the ark looked like."

"Did you have to pick the one and only time God decided to wipe out mankind from the face of the earth?" you ask, sorta joking and sorta not. "I mean, couldn't we have seen Joseph and his coat of many colors? Or what about Moses? The parting of the Red Sea would've been nice. Or maybe hearing Jesus preach?"

"You shoulda come with me in the first place," Phil tells you.

"Have you met Noah?"

Phil puts a hand over your mouth. "Shh."

"What?"

Your father shakes his head. "He's a bit—well, saying he's intense just doesn't do it justice."

"You saw him, then."

"Yes. And we don't want to see him again. He's a wild man, that Noah."

"Really?"

Phil nods. "And they say *I'm* wild."

"So you've seen the ark. Let's get out of here."

You manage to slip back out of the ark, and now you're headed away from the unruly crowd, back to the time machine. The rain is falling hard. Puddles are everywhere.

"So when'd you get here?" you ask Phil.

"Oh, I reckon it's been about five or six days. They hadn't closed up shop yet on the ark."

"So you saw all the animals."

"Every one of them," Phil says. "It was like the most amazing and messy zoo you've ever been to. Koala bears right next to lions. Some of those animals I'd never even seen before."

"I still can't believe how big that thing was."

"I hope you took some pictures of it."

You look at Phil. "What for? Are you planning on sharing them on our Facebook page or something?"

"It'd be nice to show Miss Kay."

"I was a little too busy *saving* you."

"Is that what you call it?" Phil says. "I remember you looking a little lost."

You guys reach the time machine and get back inside. You're both drenched.

"Let's go back home," Phil says.

You suddenly have this awful thought.

*John Luke. Uncle Si. Jase.*

"We have to pick all the other guys up."

"Really? And where'd they go?"

A door in the back wall of the machine swooshes open, and John Luke comes in, eating something. He's followed by Si and Jase.

"They have the most amazing puffballs in the back there," Jase says. "Each one tastes like some kind of meal. Lobster. Chicken stir-fry. Egg foo yong."

"What are you guys doing in here?" you ask.

"Man, you're wet," Si says.

"We got back in the time machine," John Luke says. "Didn't the red-haired guy explain to you how the machine works?"

You shake your head.

"Think of this as a door," Jase says as if he's trying to imitate an intelligent-sounding voice.

"This right here's the stairway to heaven, Jack," Si states.

"I'd prefer going home and getting some warm clothes," Phil says.

"So why didn't any of you come out and get us?" you ask the three of them.

"I'm not going out *there*," Jase says. "It's the end of the world."

"And we were out there," you remind him. "We could've died. Thanks to you."

"We were eating puffballs," Si says.

25

John Luke nods.

"Okay, gentlemen," Phil says. "Let's set our sails for West Monroe."

"And let's try to make it before Korie's party, okay?" you say.

"We still gotta get Mom her birthday present," John Luke says.

You nod as Jase works at one of the control panel screens.

"Do you guys have any of those puffballs left?" you ask. "Bet Korie would love them."

## THE END

# 1863

YOU STEP OUTSIDE INTO THE SUNLIGHT and for a moment are blinded. As your eyes adjust, you hear the sound of horses rushing toward you.

"There he is!"

"Over here!"

"He's alone!"

When you can see what's happening, you find yourself in a field with rolling hills around it. The men coming toward you are wearing gray outfits. Exactly like the kind the Confederates wore in the Civil War.

"Where is he?" the first man who comes up to you asks.

"Where is who?" you ask.

"You know who."

"He's the one who took the general!" a second man cries.

There's shouting all around you, and you realize that something very strange is happening.

*Could I really be here? Or are these just actors?*

But they sure don't look and sound like actors.

"He's the man who took General Jackson. Same look. Same beard."

You realize they must think you're someone else.

*Stonewall Jackson? Is that who they're talking about?*

You walk up to one of them, offering a hand, when suddenly a gun goes off nearby.

It's the last thing you'll ever hear . . .

Until you hear a female voice singing, "Yeah, yeah, yeah, yeah, yeah, yeah," and you're standing back in the warehouse, phone ringing loudly. You don't remember anything that happened, but you find yourself thinking about the Civil War for some reason.

## THE END

# TODAY

THERE'S BARELY ENOUGH ROOM for you in this confined space. You tap on the walls of the outhouse, but everything feels sturdy and unmovable. The panel of wood that you sit on doesn't move either. John Luke hasn't slipped inside it and isn't hiding.

For a second you look up at the ceiling. There's a strange little blinking light going off. Then the door shuts.

You blink, and everything changes. You're no longer in the narrow box of the outhouse. You're now standing in a room that's not square but circular. The blank, boring walls have transformed into elaborate panels full of blinking buttons. At the middle of this room—and it's a very large room—is a round control center that looks like something you'd find at Chuck E. Cheese's. It has monitors and panels and several chairs in front of it.

This totally looks like the inside of some kind of spaceship. Like something from *Star Trek* or *Doctor Who*.

"Hello?" you call out.

You're not sure if you're dreaming. Nothing around you makes sense. If this is a joke—and it no longer feels like one—then it is a very, very elaborate joke.

"John Luke?"

You hear a ticking and a whirring from the knobs and buttons on the control center. On one screen is a set of about a hundred different images. You see a bunch of photos but don't recognize any of them. Some are places and some are people. There are numbers and colors. You press one of them and feel a slight jolt.

You look around again but don't see anybody.

A siren starts to sound, and you circle around the set of monitors until you're in front of a screen that blinks with the number *1990*.

You feel a rumbling that seems to be coming from all around you. Like a car engine revving.

The number *1990* keeps blinking and seems to be getting bigger and brighter on the screen. Then another message shows up.

**YES, TOUCH THE SCREEN.**

So you do exactly what it says. The shaking continues, and you feel yourself floating and spinning around like you're on some amusement park ride. The lights all seem to blend together and blind you for a second. You can't help but pass out.

When you wake up, the outhouse is dark again. The screen you just touched isn't blinking anymore, but it still says *1990*.

*Maybe this is a time machine and I went back in time.*

You know that's not what happened, and you also know that you're surely going to wake up and find yourself asleep in a duck blind somewhere. Or maybe stretched out in your favorite reclining chair.

You hear music playing outside. You remember that you're still looking for John Luke.

The song playing outside . . . you haven't heard it for some time.

Do you head outside to find John Luke?
Go to page 59.

Do you figure this must be some kind
of jambalaya-inspired dream and hope
you wake up soon? Go to page 67.

Do you decide to stay put until you figure
out what's going on here? Go to page 15.

# TODAY

AN ALARM IS SOUNDING in the control room. As you look for the source of the noise, you spy a red warning screen flashing urgently, so you walk over to the armchair in front of the screen and read the message.

## CRISIS SITUATION

It's getting louder. Then it starts to sound like a dog barking.

The siren has turned into a barking dog.

*What kind of crazy spaceship is this?*

The screen's content changes.

## PRESS THE BUTTON, DUMMY.

Sure enough, a big, blinking button that glows and reads *Press Now* is flashing below the screen.

"Oh, okay, I'm going to press the button."

Just in case your brothers are watching you right now—and in case Raymond was some guy in on this whole joke—you look around to make sure any cameras catch you grinning, then push the button.

Now everything is moving and shaking, jerking you off your feet and onto the floor. The thing feels like it's taking off.

After a few moments, it stops and the doors open.

You stand and peer at the screen. It's still flashing on and off, but now it says something different.

**BE CAREFUL, AVOID DANGER, AND DON'T BE STUPID.**

"Okay, I sure will."

**Do you step right outside of the machine you're in?
Go to page 27.**

**Do you take the computer's advice and wait
before stepping outside? Go to page 81.**

# A LONG, LONG TIME AGO

YOU SEEM TO WAIT FOREVER, feeling your heartbeat as you hover in the darkness and shiver in your wet clothes. You keep hearing more and more voices outside, screaming and yelling and cursing. Occasionally you hear knocks—probably things being thrown at the giant boat.

You've never thought very hard about this part of the Bible, but now you know the mistake you made. It's not really a sweet story about animals for little kids. It's pretty scary. Who could live like this for long, in total darkness with the rain pounding against the boat? How many days? Forty, right?

*Forty days and forty nights.*

You've been waiting for forty minutes and you're already ready to go home.

Steps signal someone's approach. But you stay put. You see light and wonder how that can be. Then you see a shadow coming around the corner.

"Who's that?" a thunderous voice calls out.

You know it's not Phil. You think about running, but the figure is blocking your exit.

"What are you doing in here?" the man calls out when the light reveals you crouching in the corner.

"I'm not here to harm anyone."

"You're not supposed to be here."

In one hand is a lantern-like thing that's giving off the dim light. In the other is a long stick of some kind.

It sorta resembles a baseball bat.

"Look, my name is Willie Robertson, and I believe very much in the same things you folks do. I don't mean to do anybody any harm. What's your name?"

"My name is Ham, and you do not belong here."

The baseball-bat thing strikes down at you, and you're out.

• • •

Seconds or minutes or hours later—you don't know because you wake up in a puddle of rainwater with those dark skies above you—you open your eyes and feel the rain splashing on your face.

You're off the ark. The crowd surrounds you. Fights are breaking out. Some people are screaming and crying.

You still can't believe a guy named Ham took you out.

You need to come up with a plan. You need to figure out a way back onto the boat.

But first things first. You need to get dry. Maybe start a fire.

All of this is wishful thinking. You know that because you've read what happens.

Those in the boat survive.

You, however, are not in the boat.

But as soon as the water closes over your head, you find yourself back in your warehouse, with Britney Spears singing that annoying song on your phone, over and over again.

## THE END

# 1990

**"EXCUSE ME, MR. HARRIS."**

The teacher resembles a ruler in khaki pants and a button-down shirt. He sends you a nervous look.

"What if I told you I'm from the future?" You give him a big ole grin. He doesn't say a word.

"What if I said I was one of your—well, let's just say, not-so-gifted students? What if I were to tell you that one day in the future, I'd end up becoming—?"

The lights suddenly turn off.

Pitch-black.

Then you see a set of a dozen lights moving toward you like a swarm of fireflies. You suddenly feel your hands being grabbed and placed behind your back. Then you feel the cuffs. You're led out by two figures on either side of you.

Soon you're sitting in a chair with a blinding light

overhead. Figures in black helmets and black costumes stand around you.

"You breached code 746 in time code appraisal elements," one of them says.

"I what?" you ask.

"Time travel is not intended to do harm. There is an etiquette that must be observed. Just like there's etiquette in hunting."

"What harm was I doing?" you ask. "What 'etiquette' was I breaking?"

"Nor is it meant for bragging or boasting."

You shrug and laugh. "Oh, come on. That teacher tortured me. I was just going to let him know that a former student of his made it big."

"Do you think he won't know?" a low voice behind a helmet asks.

Then one of the figures hands you two pills. One is red and the other blue.

You laugh. "Ah, so I get to choose which pill I take?"

The man in black closest to you only shakes his head. "No, you take both."

"I take both?" you ask. "Really? Won't that—I don't know—do something weird?"

He attempts to force the pills into your mouth, but you wave him off and take the pills yourself.

You will never remember any of this again.

But as you find yourself standing in the warehouse with "Oops! . . . I Did It Again" playing on your cell, you have the strangest taste in your mouth.

## THE END

# TODAY

**OKAY, WAIT A MINUTE . . .**

You still have some kind of strange outhouse thing in your warehouse that John Luke *and* Jase disappeared in.

You still have no idea what's going on.

And you still have to get Korie a birthday present.

But you're heading to Duck Diner?

Really?

Come on, man. Give your stomach a break.

Yes, sure, the basketball game you played last night in your church league went into triple overtime. And yes, sure, your ankle's kind of sore. So you deserve a good meal for lunch. Maybe the meat loaf sandwich.

But there are other things happening. Strange things.

You make it halfway to Duck Diner before realizing you

should probably go back and get in that dumb contraption and see what happens.

Yeah. You'll always have a chance to eat.

But this might be your only chance to see what happens in the magical outhouse.

**Do you turn around? Go to page 55.**

**Do you go ahead and eat anyway? Go to page 103.**

# 1990

"YOU SAID THAT JOHN LUKE got in here first, right?" Jase asks. "Then disappeared?"

"Yeah."

"Well, there's a history button over there that shows where this thing has been. I bet we can push it, and it'll take us to wherever the machine was last."

"Really? What's it look like?"

"It's the big square one that says *History Button*."

You want to tell Jase to stop being annoying, but then you realize he might actually be telling the truth. So you press the button.

When the machine lands and the door opens, you realize you are definitely *not* back home in West Monroe.

"Jase, what have you done?"

That's when you see a familiar figure running toward you. "We gotta go fast!" he shouts.

It's John Luke. He darts past you, into the time machine. Behind him is what looks like some of your high school football team.

Hang on a minute. It's the entire football team. Including your high school self.

You don't wait. You bolt back through the time machine door and shut it. "Take us home, Jase!"

John Luke is sweating. He's also got a black eye and a bloody nose.

"What happened?" you ask him.

"*You*. That's what happened."

You're not sure what he's talking about (but you're not sure a lot of the time).

"Who beat you up?"

"You did," he says. "The younger version of you."

"Why?"

"Because Mom . . ." He stops.

"What?"

"No, I can't."

"What happened?"

"Mom kissed me."

"This is totally like *Back to the Future*," Jase says.

"You shouldn't have gotten the mullet," you tell John Luke.

You feel the machine starting to move and swirl around. You grab at the railing.

"We can go somewhere else," Jase says.

"Home," both you and John Luke say at the same time.

"It's giving me two options here. One is 'Duck,' and the other is 'Buck.'"

**Do you pick Duck? Go to page 19.**

**Do you pick Buck? Go to page 223.**

**Do you decide to override the system
and try to enter the current date and
West Monroe? Go to page 147.**

# ????

THE BANGING ON THE DOOR of the outhouse time machine persists. You and Si wait to see if the attackers will give up and go away, but then you hear the door rattling as if someone is trying to get inside. Soon it begins opening on its own.

"They figured it out! What are we gonna do?" you yell to Si.

"I have no idea, Jack!"

You picture the armed men tearing through the doorway with guns blazing. You steady yourself, ready to face them.

Then suddenly Phil walks through the door in his thick beard and camo-patterned bandanna, closely followed by John Luke. They do a double take when they see you, and you rub your clean-shaven face self-consciously.

"Willie, is that you? What on earth happened? What are you two doing in here?" Phil asks, still gaping at you.

"Where are *you* coming from?" you reply.

"John Luke and I have been checking out Camp Ch-Yo-Ca," Phil says.

So you must have made it back home. Both you and Si get out of the machine as fast as you can. Phil wants to know why this outhouse is here.

"Don't ask me, but take my word for it—you should stay out of it."

He believes you and gives his own beard a nervous tug as if to make sure it's still there.

You have a question too. "What were you and John Luke doing at the camp?"

"Oh, we've been looking into reports of hauntings. Spooky things. Things that go bump in the night."

The three of you are standing in front of the time machine outhouse when John Luke's cousin Cole walks over. As he takes in your hairless appearance, his shocked expression matches Phil's and John Luke's. This might take some getting used to, but still, you've never been so happy to see your family.

"Where'd you come from?" Phil asks Cole.

"Around."

You're all standing there talking when Cole decides to

rush into the outhouse. His curiosity must have gotten the best of him. Before you know it, the door shuts and the lights start going off.

Then the machine is gone.

You look around at the others. "Uh, guys, what just happened?"

"I think Cole stole the time machine," Uncle Si says.

"I hope he can figure out how to work it better than I could," you say.

"I think we lost Cole," John Luke says. "Forever."

All of you stand around as if the outhouse is going to appear again. As if you'll have another chance to get inside and find a huge room where you can go to other worlds.

"Maybe we should keep looking at what's happening around here," John Luke says.

"Of course," Phil tells him. "Gentlemen, there's a mystery to be solved. John Luke and I have important work to do."

That said, Phil and John Luke head out to return to camp. You and Uncle Si just look at one another.

*This is weird.*

"Well, Uncle Si, we got a massive order in and gotta get back to work."

He licks his finger and aims it at your ear.

"That only works when you're invisible."

He claps his hands twice as he turns in a circle. "I'm invisible now, right?"

You're not sure if he's being funny or not.

With Uncle Si, you never know exactly what he's saying.

## THE END

# TODAY

YOU PULL OUT YOUR PHONE and dial your wife. She always knows what to do. "Hey, Korie—are the guys playing some kind of practical joke on me?"

She's out of breath after finishing up her yoga workout. "What do you mean?"

"There's some kind of—well, there's an outhouse in my warehouse. And it's got, like, antennas on it."

"What are you talking about?" Korie asks.

"I'm not sure. That's why I'm calling you."

"I don't know anything about it."

You think for a moment about mentioning how John Luke and Jase disappeared, but then decide against it. You'll keep that to yourself. You know, just in case something actually *did* happen to them.

There's always your brother Jep to blame.

"Okay, well, if you hear anything, text or call me, okay?" you say.

"Shouldn't you be shopping?"

You laugh. "What for? Anything special going on?"

"John Luke told me that's what he was doing over lunch."

"Yeah, well . . ."

"What?" Korie asks.

"Oh, nothing. We're just—well, I can't say."

"Don't be planning anything big, okay?"

*I'm hoping to find our son.*

"Okay. I won't. I promise. Love ya."

Just as you hang up with Korie, you see Uncle Si sauntering down the hallway.

"Si," you call out. "What's this all about?"

"That thing right there is a time machine if I ever saw one."

"What?"

"Yeah," he says. "Got a control panel and antennas. 'Beam me up, Scotty.'"

"Who put it here?"

"Martians. Or maybe it's Bruce Willis."

"Seriously, Si."

He examines the door and the duck-shaped opening in the front.

"You didn't see any butterflies come out, did you?"

"Nope."

"'Cause you know, if you kill *one* butterfly during time travel, you can end all humanity as we know it."

Uncle Si, as usual, is full of "interesting" facts. You have no idea where he comes up with this stuff.

"Si—did you learn that in 'Nam?" you ask. "Considering I haven't stepped foot in the thing yet, I think we'll be okay."

He presses the button to open the door and steps inside. "Look at that. Hey—maybe it'll be like *Phil & Ed's Awesome Adventure*."

"I think you're talking about Bill and Ted. And it's *excellent*, not *awesome*."

"Excellent, awesome, that's what's gonna happen when I travel in time."

Before you can try to hold the door open, it shuts with Si still in there.

The lights flash—this time they're pink and yellow—and a whirring engine sound fills your ears. Then it stops.

The door opens. And, yep. Just like the last two times . . . *No Si.*

"This is ridiculous."

You circle the outhouse for about the tenth time.

Hopefully whoever is doing this and filming it is having

a good ole time. You look up to the ceiling and wave in case the camera's up there.

"Hey, y'all. Hope you're having fun *time traveling*."

You stand by the door of the outhouse. Are you ready to step inside and close the door?

**If you're finally brave enough to get in the outhouse, go to page 11.**

**If you're still a sissy and think it's a setup, then really . . . why don't you take your blanket and go to bed? Or maybe just turn to page 179.**

# 1990

**THE FIRST THING YOU NOTICE** when you step out the door is a row of old lockers. But not any old lockers. These are the ones they got rid of five years after you graduated.

Hold on there.

Yeah, that's right. You're walking into your old school, West Monroe High, which looks the way it did when you graduated. The way it did in, oh, let's say around 1990.

You stop for a second. Music is playing from the gym that's just down the hallway. You turn and see the outhouse standing just like it was in your warehouse. This is clearly not some elaborate prank your brothers are playing on you after all. This is real. You are really here at West Monroe High School.

A group of girls passes you by, and it's obvious that either this really is 1990 or you're at the best Halloween high school dance ever. The girls have poufy hair that surely took cans of hair spray to put up. Their dresses are bright with shoulder pads that are as big as their hairdos.

The year 1990 was like an eighties child having an identity crisis. Everything still felt so eighties, yet it was a whole new decade.

You follow them toward the gym and hear a song playing. "'Never gonna give you up,'" the voice sings.

*I've just been rickrolled.*

Of course, back then, Rick Astley was just a singer. The Internet wasn't even around. There wasn't a YouTube full of videos to rickroll in the first place.

You check your phone, but naturally it doesn't have a signal. It would be fun to text Korie from 1990.

*Guess where I am, Korie! Want me to get something out of your locker? Wonder if I can bring something back with me. Maybe it can be your birthday present!*

Yeah, you remember that you still have to get it. Maybe you can go out and buy something that would normally cost hundreds of dollars. Now, in the year 1990, it may cost only a fraction of that. Think of the savings!

What about hitting up the local toy store for some action figures and other collectibles?

You've already got a big collection of toys, many that you bought back from your kids after they received them for Christmas or their birthdays. They're still in the original boxes and are worth something. Maybe you could head to the local Walmart and buy a bunch of G.I. Joes or Cabbage Patch dolls or whatever's the latest craze now.

*Wait a minute . . . I'm supposed to be finding John Luke here. Not adding to my toy collection.*

As you near the entrance to the gymnasium, you see a group of guys you remember well. The Billowby brothers, Henry and Ralph, standing there with a couple of other kids.

The Billowby brothers were the bullies of West Monroe High. Henry was in your class and Ralph a year behind him. They still look smug with their thick, wavy hair and the leather jackets they wore everywhere, even to high school dances. The two other guys they're with are in tuxedos.

This isn't just any dance. It must be prom.

You've gone back in time to your high school prom.

This is crazy.

But what's even crazier is that you want to stop and have a nice little chat with the Billowby brothers. You can still remember Henry beating up your best friend on this night.

You'd already taken Korie home, so everything happened after you left the dance.

The big incident everybody still talks about to this day. You have an idea. . . .

**Do you stop to have a little "chat" with Henry Billowby and his gang? Go to page 129.**

**Do you decide your idea isn't very smart and you should find John Luke and figure out how to get back home? Go to page 79.**

# TODAY

THAT'S *EXACTLY* WHAT THEY WANT—to get you inside this thing. Maybe they want to lock you up in there. Maybe they'll fill it with something once you're stuck and can't escape.

*A fire hose through the duck-shaped opening in the door . . .*

*A swarm of nasty bugs that will get all over me . . .*

*A fart bomb that will make me pass out.*

Oh no. You're staying put.

You're going to stand out here and wait.

John Luke is surely part of the prank. And you have to give it to them—it's a good one.

So you wait.

Ten minutes later, you hear the shuffling of feet. You see the familiar cap belonging to your older brother Jase.

"A-plus job," you tell him.

He just walks up to you while staring at the outhouse.

"That is the weirdest thing I've ever seen," he says.

"So where'd you guys get it?"

Jase gives you an innocent look. The thing with your brother—the difference between him and John Luke—is that he has a great poker face. But you know he's lying. He has to be. He's gotta be the one up to this.

"I've never seen this."

"Sure you have," you say.

"I swear. I've never seen it. This has to be the ugliest outhouse I've ever laid eyes on."

"John Luke just got inside."

"He's in there?" Jase asks.

"No. He disappeared. Like a magic trick."

"You serious?"

He's examining the outhouse and asking questions similar to the ones you have about the antennas and the control panel on the front. Soon he manages to open the door.

"John Luke?" Jase asks.

But no John Luke.

"You guys want to get me inside that thing," you tell him.

"I've never seen it in my life."

He's really sounding believable.

Jase steps into the small enclosure. You watch and wait for something to happen.

The door slams shut. And once again the lights start flashing.

*Here we go again. Magic time!*

The lights are different colors from before. One is purple and the other is orange. You wait for them to stop. When they do, you open the door. No sign of Jase when you put your head inside.

*Of course Jase would be gone. How wonderful. How convenient.*

Once again you're on your own. The magic show is continuing, and you're the audience.

So you have a few options here.

Do you get inside and close the door to see
what happens? Go to page 15.

Do you stay outside and call Korie?
Go to page 55.

Do you feel your stomach rumbling and decide to
grab a bite to eat at Duck Diner? Go to page 45.

# A LONG, LONG, *LONG* TIME AGO

YOU WAIT FOR A FEW MOMENTS, blinking and shaking your head, knowing you gotta wake up sometime.

Instead, the door shuts. The room begins shaking. You feel motion underneath your feet. You hang on to a handle on the wall as everything shudders for a minute. Then it stops again.

*Uh-oh.*

Maybe the magic trick is over and you're back in the warehouse now. But the door opens—and you hear wildlife outside. *Lots* of wildlife.

You peer around the entrance and find yourself in the woods. No, scratch that. This is some kind of jungle. Like the Amazon jungle with thousand-year-old trees surrounding you.

You step out and decide to find out where you are.

An inner voice says you shouldn't, but you guess the door will close again and you might just find yourself in some other place.

You've been hunting before in some wild places, but nothing like this. The birds seem louder, the movement all around you more active. You see some monkeys moving just a little ways from you.

You walk for a good hour or more until you reach a break in the trees.

Then you see them.

There has to be at least half a dozen of them.

*Are those called brontosauruses? What's the other name?*

You feel like you're in *Jurassic Park*, seeing these towering dinosaurs. But they're right there, in the field in front of you. These glorious, amazing creatures. So beautiful. So serene.

*I think that one might be a brachiosaur.*

You're mesmerized and barely hear the sounds of the jungle clearing behind you. When you turn, you notice another dinosaur.

This one is a Tyrannosaurus rex.

It's beautiful too. But angry.

Really angry.

Whoa . . . he's coming toward you!

And the next thing you know . . .

You find yourself back in the warehouse, back holding your cell phone in your hand, back getting some love from Britney Spears.

And in one piece.

No longer an appetizer for Sir T. Rex.

## THE END

# 2319

*SO THIS IS THE YEAR 2319.* You're still trying to wrap your mind around it. The time machine seems to have adjusted itself at some point—either that or you haven't been very observant. There's a door you've never noticed before at the back of the control room. When you press a square button on the side of the wall, the door slides up and leads to a hallway lined with doors similar to the one you just passed through. They're all marked:

**Medieval Times**

**Skateboards and Bikes**

**Mongol Empire**

**World War II**

**Dystopian World Outfits and Guns**

You stop at that last one. *Dystopia.* That's like a really bad future world—you learned all about it from *The Hunger Games.* Better open the last door and see what's inside, just in case that's the sort of world you're in right now.

It's a small room with futuristic rifles and handguns hanging on the wall and a couple of tables filled with matching attire. You pick out this really large cannon-like rifle with three barrels. You also decide to put on a black outfit that's made of some heavy material. Maybe it's flame resistant. Or bullet resistant. Or laser-death-fire resistant.

You head to the main room of the time machine and peer outside. It appears to be nighttime since you can see nothing except burning buildings in the distance and lights streaming from the skies. But your immediate surroundings don't seem too threatening (for the moment). So you exit and start to examine where you are.

It's definitely some kind of battleground. You pass by burned, overturned trucks every few steps. Lots and lots of wreckage can be seen. The field you're in looks like a junkyard filled with heaps of charred metal.

You hear gunfire up ahead and try to stay down. The massive rifle you're carrying is heavy.

When you've been outside for about twenty minutes, four piercing floodlights come on all around you, blinding

you momentarily. You hold your hand in front of your face and blink until you can see it again.

Then you hear a menacing voice, magnified from a distance.

"Drop your weapons and come out into the open, or we'll detonate the car you're standing beside. Come out *right now.*"

You realize you probably don't have any options. Unless . . .

*Wait, is this one of those moments I get to choose something?*

But no—it's not.

You toss your rifle to the ground and lift your hands.

Suddenly a swarm of people surrounds you. They're wearing helmets and metallic gear with large blaster-like rifles. Someone puts you in cuffs.

"Look, I'm not going to hurt—"

Something hard slams against the back of your head. You have a hard head, but not *that* hard.

All you see is darkness.

• • •

When you open your eyes once again, you see four small walls around you. You're seated at a table, your arms trapped in an immense synthetic-wood block that renders them immobile.

Soon the door opens and a woman comes in. She's wearing a military outfit of some kind.

"State your name, your vital link, and the quadrant you've come from."

*Vital link? Quadrant?*

"My name's Willie Robertson," you start to say, not sure what to do next.

**Do you tell them the whole truth?**
**Go to page 221.**

**Do you try to make up a story?**
**Go to page 151.**

**Do you decide to make a joke?**
**Go to page 177.**

# A LONG, LONG TIME AGO

YOU'RE NOT SURE why you'd need a life jacket in the middle of a desert like this, but why not? Maybe there's water involved in whatever challenge you'll be facing. When you exit the time machine, rain has started to fall. You put the life jacket under your arm and start walking down the track-covered road.

After a few miles you arrive in a village unlike anything you've ever seen.

To call it an ancient civilization wouldn't be right. Because there's no civilization here. You see only archaic huts and people in strange, rustic clothing. You try to talk to them, but nobody will respond to you. They all look at you with fear and trepidation.

The rain continues to beat down, so you go underneath a small covering suspended between two trees.

You feel like you're on the show *Survivor*.

The rain continues all night. You'd like to say that someone lets you come into their hut, but no.

The next day it's worse. You're shivering and wondering when the downpour is going to stop.

This is the day you hear someone talk about Noah.

*"No . . . ,"* you begin, and then you say, *"ah."*

You begin to understand a little about the choices you were given.

"Where is this Noah?" you ask a big man with more hair than you.

He only mumbles and shoves you down. The woman you ask next reluctantly tells you Noah is on the boat in the hills.

"The boat in the hills. Where are the hills?"

She points in the opposite direction from where you came. "It's too dark to see them now, but you'll find them if you head that way."

You wonder if your father is on that boat in the hills. Otherwise known as the ark.

You peer through the rain. Then you put on your life jacket and begin the trek toward the vessel.

You do make it to the massive boat in the hills, and it's more spectacular and incredible than you ever could have imagined.

You're not the only one who journeyed to the ark. As each day passes and as the voices around you cry out, only to go unheard, you feel a bit of hopelessness coming on.

As it turns out, the life jacket would be okay if you fell off a boat into the lake. But when it comes to gushing skies and turbulent, swaying floodwaters, a life preserver is like a flyswatter against Godzilla.

You end up lasting longer than you would without the jacket, but not much.

And oops . . . there you go again.

You're in the familiar warehouse, standing again, breathing again. Wondering what just happened.

Wondering why in the world you're soaking wet.

## THE END

# 1990

YEAH, PROBABLY A GOOD THING not to pick a fight with guys half your age. It could get ugly.

You walk off toward the gym. You're getting lots of looks. But it's okay—you're not doing anything abnormal. It's just that here, people are wondering who in the world you are. Most places, people already know who you are, and they look anyway. At least nobody's gonna come up and make you pose for a selfie with them.

Back in 1990, there was no such thing as a selfie.

*And the world was a better place because of it.*

As you enter the gym, you notice a DJ near the back of the room. He's actually playing records. That's so vintage and cool.

You scan the crowd but can't see John Luke.

*What about Korie? What about me?*

The two of you, age eighteen, are somewhere in this building. Maybe dancing. Maybe talking with friends.

You get this crazy idea in your head as you watch the DJ.

What if you requested a song? Your song, the one Korie and you always sing when you're doing karaoke.

You smile.

Or . . . what if you introduced the teens of West Monroe High to one of the greatest dance crazes ever to hit YouTube?

You know you have to find John Luke. But sometimes in life you also gotta have fun. Especially if you've actually landed back at your prom.

**Do you decide to be responsible and find John Luke?**
**Go to page 87.**

**Do you decide to play your karaoke song?**
**Go to page 91.**

**Do you introduce the students to one of the greatest dance crazes ever? Go to page 207.**

# 1863

YOU DON'T STEP OUT of the machine at first. You wait, something you don't always like to do. But from where you stand, squinting out of the duck-shaped opening in the door, you realize this thing you're in—the outhouse—is resting in an open field. In the distance, you notice a group of men on horses. They're dressed like Confederate soldiers.

Maybe this is one of those places that does war reenactments.

Regardless, you think they'll start coming your way at any moment. But they don't. They pass several hundred yards away as if they don't see the machine.

*Maybe they don't.*

Once they're gone, you take a step out into the sunlight. As your eyes adjust, you hear the sound of a duck call—the

Duck Picker, to be exact. You realize it must be Jase since no one else can do that call so well.

You turn toward it and see him riding a horse behind another Confederate soldier. This one's wearing a fancier and darker uniform than the men who passed by earlier. His face looks tough under his cap, and his beard makes him seem like he'd be at home at Duck Commander.

"I finally got him!" Jase yells.

When he pulls up next to you, Jase is out of breath. He's somehow wearing a Confederate soldier's uniform too. But he still has his signature shades on.

"How'd you get that?" you ask.

"I've been here for a week. What took you so long?"

You shrug and try to figure out how Jase could have been in the 1800s for that many days. "A week? What are you talking about?"

"That machine—the one you just traveled in. It's a time machine. Didn't you meet the big redheaded guy? Long hair and a beard?"

You nod. "Yeah."

"He's like the time travel guru. Didn't really tell me how to work the thing, but he said you can't actually die during time travel because things would get messed up, so yeah. You'll just end up back at home, I guess. Nice to know."

"Uh-huh. Hey, is John Luke around here somewhere?"

"Don't think so, man. Haven't seen him."

How are you going to find John Luke when he could be anywhere in time or space? "Where are we right now?"

"This is Spotsylvania County in Virginia. It's April 29, 1863."

"So let me get this right," you say, staring at your brother on the horse. "You chose to go back to the Civil War?"

"Absolutely."

"What kind of idiot gets to travel in time and goes back to *the Civil War*? Do you want to die?"

The Confederate soldier on horseback, who's been watching you in silence all this time, clears his throat before interrupting. "I will not tolerate this any further!"

He's got a commanding voice with a deep Southern drawl. You know he's gotta be someone important.

"Go your own way and I will not follow you," the man says.

"Do you know who this is?" Jase asks you.

You look at the face and swear you've seen this man before. He looks like someone you don't want to mess with.

"I keep tellin' him I'm savin' his life," Jase says.

Your brother hops off his horse and tries to help the soldier off too, but the guy doesn't let him. He insists on dismounting on his own.

"Tell him who you are," Jase says to the man.

The man has animated eyes that don't fit with his sad, stern face. "My name is Lieutenant General Thomas Jonathan Jackson, commander of the second corps of General Robert E. Lee's Army of Northern Virginia. And I demand to be let go."

Jase looks like he just made the biggest catch of his life.

"Wait a minute," you say. "Are you Stonewall Jackson? General Stonewall Jackson?"

"Yes."

You're not quite an expert on history here, but you try to remember what happened.

"Isn't . . . ? Where are we at?" you ask.

"Near the village of Chancellorsville."

The commanding way the man speaks would be enough to encourage you to take a gun and go into battle.

*This is General Stonewall Jackson.* The *Stonewall Jackson.*

You almost ask him for an autograph before realizing something.

"Uh, Jase—hey, uh, come over here for a minute."

You step away from Jackson and begin to whisper so he can't hear you.

"Do you know what's about to happen?" you ask in a soft voice.

"Of course I do! The Battle of Chancellorsville."

"You can't change history. What do you think you're doing?"

Jase laughs. "Exactly what you think I'm doing."

"And how'd you get that costume?"

"It's real, and that's really Stonewall Jackson."

"Then that means it's really 1863!"

"Yes, it does," Jase says. "And I think I'm gonna help General Jackson here."

Somehow time travel has made Jase's brain shrink.

"You do know that you can't rewrite the past," you tell him. "I mean—I know you're all into the Confederate flag and all that, but a lot of good things happened when the South lost."

Jase clearly doesn't want to listen. He's caught up in the moment.

You have to make a decision—and fast. The future as you know it might be forever changed.

*Why didn't I study history a little better?*

Do you keep the general in your possession for
the moment and hope you can figure out a plan
to ditch him later? Go to page 133.


Do you force Jase to let Stonewall Jackson
go, then make him get back in the time
machine with you? Go to page 141.

# 1990

**YOU DECIDE TO KEEP SEARCHING FOR JOHN LUKE.**

The song changes to "Pour Some Sugar on Me," and you see a kid on the dance floor rocking out while his mullet hairstyle rocks with him. You shake your head. You know you had the same style for quite a while.

*Wait, maybe I still had the mullet back in 1990!*

You scan the crowd of a hundred students dancing and look for someone not dressed up. But John Luke is nowhere to be found. You do see your old gym teacher and the chemistry teacher. You wonder if they're going to recognize you.

*Of course they won't.*

An adult chaperone—possibly someone's mother—approaches you, and you say you're a relative of the Robertson boys. The chaperone nods at your explanation but makes it clear she's going to be keeping a careful watch on you.

Where would John Luke be right now?

You walk the perimeter of the gym, the lights dimmed to add mood to the dance floor. You're about to make it around the entire floor when you see a figure you haven't thought of for years.

Samantha Price.

The quiet girl who, you remember, was always nice to everybody but had the great misfortune of dating Rick Hoight her junior and senior years. Until she got dumped.

*Like on this very night.*

Samantha is still at the dance, but why, you don't know. You wouldn't have known back in high school either, but of course you didn't pay attention to her then. You were young and busy and in love.

Something about seeing Samantha breaks your heart.

You would learn after graduating that Rick broke up with Samantha at prom in favor of some younger girl. Then he'd dump that girl and try to win Samantha back. But she was smart enough to say no.

She's not with her friends because they're on the dance floor.

So is Rick. He's dancing with his new girl for the night.

You realize you have this strange opportunity to do something for her. But what? What could you possibly do for Samantha?

Do you decide not to get distracted and keep trying to find John Luke? Go to page 113.

Do you come up with an idea to make Samantha's night? Go to page 165.

# 1990

YOU WALK OVER TO THE DJ.

"Do you have 'Love Shack' by the B-52s?"

He gives you a real cool-guy nod.

"Can you play it next?"

He just gives you another nod, his mushroom-shaped hair bouncing.

"That's, like, the go-to karaoke song for me and my wife."

"Your go-to what?" he asks.

"You know—the song we always pick when we kar-a-o-ke."

Then it dawns on you that this guy hasn't heard of karaoke. It hasn't become a thing yet. "Never mind," you mutter and step away.

*Man, I'm old.*

You stand on the side of the gym, watching the dancers,

and that's when you see her. The smiling girl in the black dress. You notice that the dress is really puffy, just like her hair, but other than that your future wife looks so cute.

*Is it weird to be thinking this?*

You decide to surprise her on the dance floor. It's gonna be awesome.

Soon the music begins to play.

Those drums start, and then you hear the wail of *"Love shack!"*

Everybody is out on the floor dancing, including Korie and her friends. So you join them. Who cares if you're from the future and a little older than everybody else. You're only as old as you feel. Right?

You close your eyes and start dancing. You know all the lyrics, and you're soon mouthing the words.

You do motions with your hands and twist your hips. You're wearing boots, but that's okay—you can do your best moves in them.

That's right. You've still got it.

*"Love shack, bay-bee."*

You finally open your eyes and look around.

The entire room is staring at you.

Everybody's glaring, and nobody's dancing.

You slowly stop dancing as you realize the students might be a little confused. Or maybe sorta scared.

*So they've never seen a bearded man with a bandanna who can move and groove so well.*

You try to sneak off the basketball court and out of the gym. The dancing resumes.

Before leaving, you feel something hit your head. It's a dress shoe. You don't even bother to check who threw it.

"Love Shack" was a total disaster.

You decide to wait for John Luke by the time machine, which is fortunately still here. Then you two can go back to 2014 and break out the karaoke machine, and you and Korie can bust out "Love Shack" tonight.

Right now you feel a bit like a fool.

You're forty-two years old and a 1990s prom has defeated you.

*"Bang, bang on the door, baby."*

## THE END

# A LONG, LONG
# TIME AGO

**WHEN THE FIRST OF THE RAINS COME,** you feel good. It's cool and refreshing outside. But that's until it rains all day and all night. Then it keeps raining. And raining.

It rains more.

And more.

The rains keep coming.

The storms get heavier.

When you talk to a guy from a nearby town, you realize the man in the cloak must have been right about something bad happening out here. The local guy mentions a man named Noah who predicted this very thing.

But by the time you hear about this, it's too late. The waters rise, and even though you're a good swimmer, you can't swim forever.

And the rains seem to go on forever.

You should have followed the cloaked man's advice.

But then you remember what he said about not dying, and your predicament doesn't seem so bad after all.

Sure enough, soon you're standing in the middle of the familiar warehouse, confused, dripping wet, and listening to Britney Spears singing "Oops!" at full volume on your phone.

## THE END

# TODAY

SO HERE'S THE GOOD NEWS: you and Jase make it back home to West Monroe in time for Korie's birthday.

The bad news: John Luke never shows up.

The really bad news: you left the time machine in the warehouse when you got home from the Civil War, but now it's gone. You have no idea where to find it.

John Luke is missing and Korie is worried and you have no idea how in the world you're going to let her know her eldest son is now trapped somewhere in another time and another place.

But you're definitely going to blame Jase.

That's the *last* time he's ever going to do something you tell him to do!

## THE END

# 1990

YOU TRY TO TALK TO KORIE, but she runs down the hallway. Literally *runs*.

You try again and she steps behind a group of girlfriends.

You try for a third time and she goes over to Mr. Harris, one of the teachers standing nearby. He walks over to you.

"May I help you, sir?"

Then something dawns on you.

You're a forty-two-year-old trying to talk to an eighteen-year-old. That's creepy enough.

Then there's the beard and the bandanna that nobody's ever seen. You surely look a little bit . . . scary.

"Oh yeah, sorry. I was just trying to find my son."

"Somehow I don't think Korie Howard is your son."

You realize Mr. Harris is around the same age as you. This is the same Mr. Harris who kicked you out of class for putting chalk in his soup one day during home ec. The same teacher who loves to belittle you in front of the entire class. Sure, you maybe deserved to be punished for the chalk incident, but Mr. Harris always seemed to take things too far.

*Hmm.*

You've often imagined meeting up with Mr. Harris again. Just to have a nice conversation. Not to hurt him. You'd never do that. But you wouldn't mind messing with his head.

Just a little.

Of course, you really should find John Luke. You're not sure if the time machine is still here, or how in the world you guys will be able to get back.

**Do you stay and mess with Mr. Harris's mind?**
**Go to page 41.**

**Do you go into the gym, hoping John Luke**
**will be there? Go to page 87.**

# NOVEMBER 22, 1963

**WAIT A MINUTE . . .**

How'd you get *here*?

Did you cheat?

You wouldn't do something like that, would you?

And if you would, you wouldn't pick such a predictable date, right?

You do know there were multiple gunmen, don't you?

Are you really going to save the president? What's your plan?

Oh, wait; you didn't know you'd end up here?

Are you saying you don't even know what happened on this date?

Okay, that's fine. Just go back to the beginning and start over. (And look up this historical date when you get a moment!)

# WILLIE'S REDNECK TIME MACHINE

**Start over on page 1.**

# TODAY

YOU DECIDE TO GO ON and eat because you do your best thinking while eating. After polishing off a fried shrimp po'boy sandwich, you go to use the men's room before leaving Duck Diner. When you walk inside, you see the strangest thing.

The outhouse is *in* the men's restroom. It barely fits too.

You have *no* idea how someone fit a giant wooden outhouse in your restaurant's bathroom.

You think about turning around and talking to the manager. But enough's enough. You get it. They want you to hop in. They *really* want to get you inside. So okay.

"All righty, boys," you say out loud.

You're sure that someone's got a camera on you, watching. This will make the Jimmy Kimmel show or *America's*

*Funniest Home Videos* or maybe a country music award show. Who knows.

You step inside, close the door, and wait.

Will the floor open up to something?

Will they fill the outhouse with something gross or funny?

Will the . . . ?

You blink. Something's strange about your surroundings. You blink again and realize you're not making this up.

The outhouse has changed into some kind of spaceship. And just as you're about to walk across the floor to figure out how this happened, the room starts spinning.

Violently.

You try to hang on to something but can't. You're launched across the room into the wall, then to the floor.

As you slide, you grab the base of a chair, managing to grip it until the shaking and spinning stops.

Sirens are going off, and when you eventually stand up, you see one thing flashing across all the screens in the room (and there are lots of them):

## 2038

It looks like that's a year. Yeah, you're smart to notice stuff like that.

You try to get your bearings. You feel the shrimp po'boy sandwich rumbling around in your stomach. Maybe you shouldn't have had that along with those fried pickles.

*But how can anybody resist the fried pickles? Come on, now.*

So maybe you're in a time machine.

Maybe you're supposed to embark on some great adventure. It's not enough that you're a secret agent (and nobody knows about that)—

*Oh, wait; that's another story.*

You get to the door, and it opens easily. So you step out, unsure what you'll discover.

You find you're in another restroom. This one happens to be in a Walmart store. You're heading to the exit when something catches your eye. It's the store logo.

Duck Commander has done lots of business with Walmart over the years, so you know its logo well. But this . . . this isn't it.

There's a *W* and an *A* side by side.

Right underneath it, you see the word *Walmazon*.

*What in the world?*

You spot the customer service desk and swing by it.

"So what's with Walmazon?" you ask.

The girl behind the desk looks confused.

"When did it change from Walmart?"

"From what?" the young girl says.

Someone else comes up behind her. It's an older man with lots of gray hair around the sides of his head.

"That was like . . . like in about 2020 or '21. That's going back old-school. Yeah, the big merger between Walmart and Amazon. Basically changed shopping as we know it."

You should have seen that one coming! You nod and thank the man.

"Hey—nice look. I remember that family. Who were they again? The Robinsons?"

You're not sure if he's trying to be funny.

"Robertsons," you say.

"Oh yeah. Something about ducks and stuff, right?"

You nod again and leave the desk.

That was weird.

You step out of Walmazon and wonder what you're supposed to do. Shopping in the future sure doesn't sound like an adventure to you.

A tiny red car with big wheels pulls up to the curb. It's round, and you're not sure you can even fit into it. A man with glasses and a goatee is driving. He's wearing a bow tie and one of those blazers that surely has elbow patches on it.

"Hey, Dad," the man says. "Get in."

You look for a moment before you recognize the face.

*John Luke?*

"I know. It's crazy, huh? I'm forty-two years old. The same age as you."

Now you really study him. "Love the jacket. And the whole look."

"Come on," John Luke says.

His voice is lower than you're used to.

"How did you know—?"

"Because you told me in the past to be watching for you today."

You think for a minute. "But how does that work? Did I come back from the future to tell you that? Or did my past self journey to the future to tell you?"

"Remember when there was such a thing as texting?" John Luke says through the window. "Imagine sending a text to me in 2038."

"So it really is 2038?"

He nods. "Come on. I'll show you around. Lots of things have changed."

**Do you get in the minicar? Go to page 201.**

**Do you run back into Walmazon and try to get in the time machine again? Go to page 185.**

# 1990

SO YOUR WIFE and your son are out there on the dance floor, but only one of them knows the truth.

*Looks like Korie thinks John Luke is me . . . otherwise she's got eyes for someone else, and that's not good. I should stop this now.* You decide to break up the weird situation by asking them if you can take their picture.

"Dad," John Luke calls out.

Thankfully Korie doesn't hear it, as she's distracted by a friend who just came over.

"Where'd you get the tux?" you ask him.

"I rented it this afternoon. Thought it'd be fun to go to an old prom. *Until now.*"

John Luke mouths the last two words, acting as if he's trapped with Korie, who joins your conversation.

"What is that?" she asks, pointing to your phone.

"Oh, just a new camera. Okay, you two, pose."

John Luke puts an arm around his future mother, and you take a few pictures.

"Thanks. Oh, uh, I'm going to need to borrow him for a minute," you tell Korie.

"What's going on?" she asks, looking at John Luke but clearly thinking he's you—er, 1990 you.

High school Willie, of course, is probably somewhere looking for his date. Things will surely get weird if the past you sees the future you along with your son, who *looks* like you did back in 1990.

*This is confusing me. I need something to eat to sort things out.*

Maybe seeing your past self will violate some kind of space-time continuum thing. You don't know. You may be an expert on duck calls and running Duck Commander, but definitely not on time travel.

"He'll be *right* back," you tell Korie.

You look at her and can't believe how cute she is. You also can't believe how puffy her sleeves happen to be.

*What was fashion thinking with those things?*

As you walk away with John Luke, he begins to explain what happened.

"I got into that—that machine—and the door closed, and all of a sudden I'm going back in time."

"So then why didn't it disappear in my warehouse?" you ask.

"I don't know. Maybe it's not a real machine—like a vehicle or something—but more like a doorway."

You stop for a minute. "John Luke—you went *back* in time and got smarter."

He's about to respond when, blocking your path to the exit from the gym, there stands the high school version of you.

Looking all tough in his tuxedo and black tie, he glares at John Luke as if he wants to fight. The good thing is that you know yourself, and you know you'd never hit someone unless they really deserved it. The bad thing is he looks like he might sock John Luke in the nose.

"Okay, hold on now," you begin.

**Do you say something meaningful to your younger self? Go to page 137.**

**Do you grab John Luke and sprint to the time machine? Go to page 173.**

# 1990

YOU CAN SEE THEM in the crowd from where you stand by a set of tables. It's Korie trying to move closer to her dance partner. But her dance partner happens to be John Luke, who looks like he might pass out in that tux he's wearing.

You have to blink to make sure it's him. He looks so much like you did back in 1990.

*Poor kid,* you think.

His mother has no idea who she's dancing with.

You weren't planning to get a photo of them, but this opportunity is too good to pass up. So, hoping that Korie will assume you're some sort of hired photographer and that John Luke won't make a scene, you get them to pose side by side and snap a picture. John Luke sends you a you'll-pay-for-this look over Korie's shoulder as they resume their dance.

You move away and watch for a few moments until someone else comes out on the dance floor.

It's you. Well, not you now, but you back in 1990.

*I was a handsome guy.*

You're feeling pretty good until you see your younger self come and say a few things to the dancing couple, then take a swing at John Luke.

Now you decide to get out there on the dance floor. Fast. Before any blood is spilled.

You're the first adult to get to the two guys. John Luke is covering his face to shield it from the punches.

"Hold on there, son," you say.

You're calling yourself "son." Time travel irony.

"Who are you, pops?"

"Easy, killer," you say. "We're just leaving."

"This guy is trying to steal my girl."

"Nobody's stealing anything, right, John Luke?"

You glance at Korie, who looks perplexed. You wonder if this is messing up the space-time continuum thing.

*I gotta learn more about this time travel stuff.*

"Come on," you tell your son. Then you look to Korie and say, "Sorry to confuse you."

"Hey, man, ZZ Top went out of style," high school Willie tells you.

"ZZ Top never goes out of style," you say as you leave.

Then you realize there's one more thing you could do while you're here.

**Do you decide to try leaving something in your locker before you leave? Go to page 125.**

**Do you just get into the time machine to go back home? Go to page 173.**

# A LONG, LONG
# TIME AGO

IT'S A STRANGE THING, walking around with a chain-saw in a place you don't know. The few people you pass on the road end up running away in terror upon seeing the power tool. You call out, telling them that no, really, you're not the Texas chainsaw killer or any sort of killer whatso-ever. But none of them listen to you.

It starts to rain, which only makes things worse. Now you look like a sopping mess *and* you happen to be wielding a very deadly piece of equipment.

You reach a small village and realize this has got to be a really long time ago. The place is primitive, scattered, with only a few faces showing themselves and quickly disappear-ing back into their huts after they do.

Why have you come to this particular time and place?

Or maybe you should ask the more important question: Why did Phil come here? He has to be close by, right?

It rains through the night, and you end up going into the nearby woods for shelter. When morning comes, the cold rain seems to double down on you.

You need to find some more effective shelter.

Or maybe you should just get rid of the chainsaw.

You return to the village and knock on a door—actually not so much a door as some branches covering an opening—and the woman behind it shouts gibberish at you. For a moment you wonder if you're unable to understand this language, but it's not that. This woman is just freaked out and talking fast.

"Please go somewhere else," you finally hear her say.

So you do.

You keep trying this, door-to-door.

You feel yourself shivering and wonder why the man in the cloak back there didn't offer you a rain poncho or maybe some flint to start a fire.

Rain starts hitting you sideways. You knock at yet another hut, and this time the makeshift door opens. A big man steps out.

It's not just a big man. This is a giant.

His eyes glare at the chainsaw in your hands.

"This is just for cutting down—"

You're on the ground and don't even realize he took a swing at you until the right side of your face goes numb.

This can't be good.

You try to stand, but he picks up the chainsaw.

Oh, man.

This really can't be good.

As he studies it, though, you realize he has no earthly idea what he's holding.

You start to run toward the woods you spent the night in. This will be where you will spend the rest of your life, watching the flood come—the flood you learned so much about back in your Sunday school days.

It won't be much of a life after all.

Thankfully, time is on your side. Actually, time travel is, and you end up back in your warehouse with Britney Spears singing, "Oops! . . . I Did It Again." This may have happened before, you realize. It's like déjà vu.

Again.

## THE END

# 2319

"YOU'RE NOT TOUCHING MY HEAD," you tell Uncle Si. "Even if it looks like a melon."

"We don't have much time, Jack. They're coming."

"Then you better get me out of here."

Si heaves a sigh and opens the door behind him.

You're led through dingy, shadowy hallways and up a cracking, abandoned staircase until you get to the top of the building. Then another narrow flight of steps in near darkness leads you onto the roof.

It's even windier up here, and the rain is falling harder. As you follow Si, you catch sight of the spacecraft he's walking toward. It's long with a narrow front and two wide, multilevel wings—as if they're four or five wings all stacked up on each other.

"These things separate," Si says, touching one of the wings. "They call this ship the Spider 'cause the wings look like spider legs."

The machine doesn't appear to have much room in it.

"Can we both fit inside?"

Si nods. "Yes. There's seats for two people. You'll be back here." He taps on some kind of barrel sticking out the back and opens a door in its side. You realize with a jolt that you're supposed to crawl in there.

"In case we get followed, you shoot them."

"What's happening, Si?"

"I'll tell you once we're in the sky. You know, you go up high enough and you can still see the blue skies. But down here all you get is this rainy gray death gloom."

"So are you fighting against the rebels?"

"No, man. I'm *leading* the rebels. This is like *Terminator* land going on here. We're the guys fighting the machines."

You want to ask more, but you don't know where to start. So you take a breath and get inside the barrel compartment.

When the spacecraft starts to go up, the strangest thing happens. You don't feel anything. Your stomach doesn't turn over like you thought it might. You feel as if you're just sitting down watching the massive city get smaller and smaller.

"Isn't it amazing?" Si says. You can see him in the pilot's

seat through the opening that connects the cockpit to your compartment.

"How can you fly this thing?"

"I've been here over a year."

"Where is here?"

"This used to be Chicago. Now the country is divided into quadrants. This is quadrant four."

You glide through the clouds. So far, from the seat you sit in that turns forward and backward, you can't see anybody following you.

"How could you have been here a whole year already?"

"The time machine got blasted two seconds after I stepped foot out of it. But this time I made sure it was protected when you arrived."

"You saw?"

"Yes. And we tried getting to you before Big Brother did. This place is trippy. And it's only 2319 too. The machines are winning."

"They're machines?"

"Nah, not really. It's just bad guys controlling machines. It's not exactly like *The Terminator* or *The Matrix*. The bad guys are the rulers who are imprisoning everybody and using machines to do it."

"Uncle Si—we have to get home."

"I know. But we need to help these people."

"How are you going to do that?" you ask.

"By defeating the bad guys."

When the machine you're in lands on another rooftop, Si looks back at you before exiting.

"You can take off if you want, but I got a battle I need to win."

**Do you decide to stay and help Uncle Si win the futuristic war? Go to page 161.**

**Do you decide to find the time machine and somehow force Si to travel home with you? Go to page 235.**

# 1990

JOHN LUKE WANTED TO COME with you and see your old locker, but you pushed him back in the time machine before he could get into any more trouble.

You shut the door of the time machine and follow the familiar path to your locker. Just down the hall from the boys' room, in the middle of the *R*s in your class. Stanley Rose had a locker right next to yours and had the worst breath imaginable. Every morning you'd say, "What's up?" and he'd deliver a blast of poo in response.

That was the worst.

Here you are again, staring at your locker, trying to remember the combination.

It can't be the same, right?

But it's 1990 again. So of course it can. It's still your locker.

Your idea really could work. It's only a tiny idea that won't harm a soul and won't be a big deal.

You think of those tough early days with the family, the times when you had to work so hard for so little. You've always wanted to go back in time and just help things out a bit. Not because money is that important in life, 'cause it's not. You've always been happy with your family. God's given you guys so much.

But . . .

You could have used some help. Before you decided to work at the camp. Before Duck Commander, when you were struggling those first few years.

So you test out your memory on the locker combination. Yep. It works.

You see books tossed around and what looks like a bagged lunch with some gym shorts on top of it. Some pictures of Korie and you decorate the inside of the door. Your locker sure doesn't smell very good (but it's nothing like Stanley's breath). You dig around until you find a notebook and a pen, then open it to write yourself a note.

*Hey, Willie. This is yourself from the future.*
*Life's been good to you, buddy. Just stay strong*
*in your faith and stay close to Korie. Oh, and*
*just so you know—the Buffalo Bills never win*

*a Super Bowl. After four consecutive trips.*
*So . . . just saying.*
*And another thing. DO NOT eat the ducks*
*you shoot on Christmas morning 1998. Just don't.*

*Willie*

You take tape from the back of one of the pictures in the locker and stick the note to the door.

You head to the time machine, ready to go home. Hopefully John Luke made it back already.

You don't expect anything to be different. Maybe some of the memories you have of lean days and nights cutting back on meals will change. But still—you've done nothing wrong. Have you?

You might be telling yourself about a potential sports bet you can make. But that's all.

This is a gift from above. You're just helping yourself out a little.

You find the time machine and step in.

**Go to page 241.**

# 1990

"GOOD EVENING, GENTLEMEN."

They all start to laugh at you. Obviously they don't know who you are. Not with the beard. And maybe you've put on a little weight, but other than that you don't think you look that different from when you were in high school.

If they don't recognize you, though, you might as well use this to your advantage.

"Henry Billowby," you say with a heavy, threatening voice.

"Yes?"

Now they're not laughing. They're wondering why the guy with the long hair and beard and the big boots is standing over them looking like he might paddle any of them in a millisecond.

"Staying out of trouble?"

The kid nods.

"You want to hear something? You may not know me, but I know you. And here's my promise to you on this night. If you do anything—and I mean *anything*—that might be considered foolish, then I'm going to come find you. I know where you live. At the end of Baker Lane, right? You and your brother."

"How do you know us?" Henry asks.

"From a long time ago. Let's just leave it at that."

"So what are you gonna do, anyway?"

This is Ralph talking. Henry was always the bigger talker, but Ralph was always the one getting in more trouble.

"Ralph, Ralph. Do you know what it feels like to hold the beating heart of a dead deer?"

The boy only shakes his head while you lean toward him and stare into his eyes.

"You don't want to mess with a man who's really good at carving up things."

His eyes are big, like balloons ready to burst.

You are about to say something else, but then you see someone approaching the entrance to the gym from the other way. It's a cute, tall, skinny girl with curly hair you recognize quite well.

It's Korie. Your date for tonight.

Your date for the rest of your life.
You don't have a clue what you're going to do.

**Do you rush over to say hi to Korie?**
**Go to page 99.**

**Do you head into the gym to search**
**for John Luke? Go to page 87.**

# 1863

IT DOESN'T TAKE YOU LONG to find a Confederate deserter to switch clothes with. At first he thought he was going to be captured when he saw you with the general, so he's more than happy when all you demand is his uniform. Granted, it's a little short and tight, but that's okay. The soldier even lets you have his horse. Giddyup.

You've always wanted to be a soldier.

"Where is Robert E. Lee?" you ask Stonewall Jackson.

But he is not talking to you. Even after you've explained half a dozen times that you're from the future. They don't understand the things you know. Time travel *is* real. Well, it *might* be real one day. To Stonewall (currently Stone*face*), though, time travel is made-up nonsense.

You've decided that maybe it's okay to save Stonewall Jackson's life. But you're not trying to help the South win the war.

Saving Stonewall Jackson won't save the South.

*Or will it?* You can't access Twitter to take a poll.

"You do know we're saving your life," you tell the general. "You realize you would get shot in battle? By your own men?"

The stern-faced general doesn't reply. Jase, however, does.

"'Fat guy in a little coat,'" he sings to you.

"Shut up and let's get these horses going." The only problem is, you're not sure where to go. "Excuse me, General? What direction is Gettysburg?"

"I think that's Pennsylvania," Jase says.

"Where are we, again?"

"Virginia."

You nod.

"Are they next to each other?" Jase asks.

"You should have paid better attention in geography," you tell your brother.

Stonewall Jackson can only shake his head.

You've been riding for half an hour when two figures approach on foot. One wears a dark poncho with a cowboy hat and the other a sombrero. Both appear to be carrying holstered pistols.

"Good day, gentlemen," you say.

"Have any of you stumbled upon a man called Angel Eyes?"

"No," Jase says, looking at you. "Willie, you know who this is?"

The two men sure look familiar.

"What are your names?" Jase asks.

"You can call me Tuco," the sombrero man says with an accent. "He's Blondie."

"I'm just waiting for the music now," Jase says. "You know—the *aheeaheeaaaaaaaa*."

"We're back in time," you say. "Not in a movie." *Are there no rules to this thing?*

The guy named Blondie is talking to you now. Not only that—his gun is aimed at you. You kinda wish you had a weapon to defend yourself, even that dagger you found in the warehouse from the Thanksgiving play—not that it would do much good against a gun.

"Give us the horses," he says. "You see, in this world there's two kinds of people, my friend: those with loaded guns and those who walk. You walk."

You're about to get off your horse, but

Stonewall Jackson won't take any more of this. He begins to ride away.

Suddenly Tuco gets nervous and draws his gun too. Jase bends over and looks like he's going to jump off the horse, but the nervous bandit thinks he's doing something else.

The sound of gunfire is the last thing you hear.

Actually, it's the steady sound of drums, followed by a flute that sounds like a coyote.

*Wah, wah, wah . . .* turns into "Oops! . . . I Did It Again." All of a sudden you're in the Duck Commander warehouse, your ears echoing with the sounds of gunshots and drums.

### THE END

# 1990

"YOU'RE PRETTY HANDSOME, you know that?" you tell your high school self.

He doesn't seem that impressed or amused. More like creeped out. He's standing in front of John Luke, still looking like he might be ready to start a fight.

*A clash between the mullet heads. That's gonna be great.*

"Hey, man, can we go take a walk?"

You know he'll say yes because he—you—learned to always respect your elders.

"Yes, sir."

You vacate the crowded gym for the hallway, leaving John Luke behind. A group of students walk past and make jokes about the beard. You're used to it.

"So how're you doing tonight?"

"Fine."

"Really? You don't *look* fine."

He doesn't say anything. It's funny seeing yourself. Especially a younger and clean-shaven version of yourself.

"Can I tell you a few things? A few things about life?"

"I'm not going to do anything to the kid," he says. "Is he your son?"

You smile and nod. "Well, yes, he is."

"I'm not going to get in a fight."

"Listen—there are times you have to put up a fight for the things you believe in. But you do so in a responsible way. How you feel about Korie—that's a cool thing. Don't ever let it go, okay? She's a good lady."

He gives you a suspicious look because, of course, he has no clue who you are. Or maybe it's because you called Korie a "lady."

"I just want you to know—you're almost out of here. And you have your whole world ahead of you. Make sure you don't change. Okay? Keep the things your parents have taught you close to your heart. Trust God. There are going to be some trying times, but that's okay. You might find yourself working in an ice cream plant in a cooler all day long. Don't let that wear you down. Big things are ahead for you."

He nods. You can tell he's still trying to figure out who you are, since that's exactly what you'd do.

INXS starts to play.

"Man, I love these guys," you tell him.

"Yeah, so do I."

*This is weird.*

You have the opportunity to tell yourself anything. But you've already said enough.

"Oh, one more thing."

"Yeah?"

"One day you'll be able to rock a beard like this one. And don't let anybody fool you—people fear the beards."

You both go back into the gym, where you find John Luke being cornered by another girl: Jill Baxter.

A girl who was in love with you and started stalking you for a while.

"Let's go, John Luke."

"This is Willie Robertson," Jill says in a hands-off-he's-mine tone.

"This is my son, whom I will kill for if necessary," you say.

It's true—not that you're going to harm her. But sometimes you just need to state the obvious to those who aren't so smart.

Jill gives you a snotty look, but she also appears to be terrified of you. She disappears in the crowd.

"That girl was crazy," John Luke said.

"Sometimes the best thing you can do when a girl tells you she likes you is run. Run away as fast as you can."

So that's what both of you do.

**Go to page 173.**

# 1863

"SIR," YOU SAY, "it's an honor and a privilege to meet you, but my idiot brother does not know what he's doing."

General Stonewall Jackson stands in front of his horse while Jase shakes his head next to you.

"You're handing them the keys to the war," Jase says.

"Have you forgotten *everything* about the Civil War? Do I really need to explain why you can't just kidnap Stonewall Jackson?" You change your tone before speaking to Jackson again. "We really don't mean you any harm, sir."

The general does not look amused or impressed.

Jase appears to have a few more things to share with him. "Maybe you'll just want to be a little careful, especially when it comes to your—"

"Jase. Shut up."

You're about to drag Jase back to the time machine, but then you remember something.

*Korie's birthday present.*

"Oh, sir, can I ask one favor?"

Soon you're pulling Jase back into the outhouse while the completely confused and confounded general stares at both of you.

*He's just waiting to tell his men about us so they can take us away.*

But the time machine will be gone before that.

Once the door closes, you swat Jase on the back of his head.

"What's that for?" he asks.

"For being an idiot."

"I was trying to help General Stonewall Jackson."

"Don't you know the first rule about time travel?" you ask.

"Save Stonewall Jackson?"

"You don't go and try to kill Hitler."

Jase just shakes his head and puts his cap back on. "You got the wrong war."

"Avoid paradoxes."

Suddenly you hear knocking at the door.

"Do you know how to get back?" you ask Jase.

"There's a way to program this thing, you know. The redheaded man told me. It's right over here."

The knocking escalates to banging. They might be able to get through the door if you don't escape soon.

"Take us back home," you command Jase.

"But what about trying something else out?"

"Home. Today. I still have to find John Luke."

**Does Jase get you both back home in time for Korie's birthday party? Go to page 97.**

**Does Jase decide to take you somewhere else? Go to page 47.**

# 2319

**YOU STEP OUTSIDE.**

Really, do you need to be told the rest?

Seriously—there's an end-of-the-world sort of war going on outside your time machine, and you still step foot outside? Even after being warned?

And sure enough, you last as long as it takes to read this page.

These are your last words.

"Oh, man, I—"

Then . . .

BOOM!

POW!

*Ow!*

*Oh no.*

And you're back in the Duck Commander warehouse, your phone ringing on and on: "Oops! . . . I did it again."

## THE TRAGIC END

# ????

YOU JOIN JASE at the controls, determined to find a way home. Next to the screen displaying the Duck and Buck choices, you notice a reset button. You press it before Jase can object, and the screen changes. Now it displays the numbers 1, 2, 3, and 4. You try to get the screen to show time and place options, but you eventually give up and ask Jase how to get there.

"I don't know what this screen does," Jase says.

He presses 4 on the screen.

"Why'd you do that?"

"Why not?"

The shaking and spinning motion begins. You hang on to a chair that's fixed in place while the machine continues to tremble for a few moments. Then it stops.

"Oh, boy," you say.

"This is fun," John Luke says.

"I hope this is better than the Civil War," you tell Jase.

"There's no way to know now that you overrode the system."

"I was just trying to send us home!"

"Well, you get to go first."

"You know we're both still dressed as Confederate soldiers," you say.

Jase nods. "There's an intervention chamber in the back."

"And what's that?"

"You can explain your issue to the main computer, and many times it fixes the problem. In this case, we'll say we need our old clothes back."

Sure enough, minutes later you're wearing your old clothes once more. They appeared in a box at the back of the intervention chamber, just as Jase suggested they would.

"Now we don't stand out as much," you say.

John Luke looks at both of you and laughs.

"What?" you ask.

"Come on," Jase says. "You get out first."

You stare at them. "Who knows what story this might drop us into."

Then you step through the doorway.

**Go to page 137 . . . in *Jase & the Deadliest Hunt.***

# 2319

**"THAT HIT ON THE HEAD** made me forget my vital link and quadrant," you say. "My brain feels foggy."

"How did you get to the fields?"

"The fields. Oh yes, those. I just . . . I don't know. It's hazy."

"You should have been killed sneaking past the security barriers."

Your brain really is a bit foggy, and now you're being forced to make up a story.

"I'm not a threat," you say. "I just—I'm not sure how I got to the fields, but I was—I wasn't going after anyone."

"You had a system 5, class 20 high-velocity batter shatter in your possession. How did you get one of those?"

"You call that rifle a batter shatter?" You can't help but laugh, and the woman doesn't seem to like your laughing.

"I got it for a birthday present," you say.

"I know of people like you."

"What do you mean?"

"You're one of them. The rebels. The ones battling against the system."

Finally you start to understand. "Yes, I get it."

"You do?"

"Yes. I've seen the movies. This is a dystopian society. But that's okay. I'm fine with dystopia. Totally fine."

"Do you even know what that means?"

You nod. "Yeah. It's like—a genre, right? The bad government—I mean, the one that some people think is bad. But I'm sure it's good."

The woman slides out what looks to be some kind of CD and puts it in her palm. It begins to hover, and she speaks into it.

"This is a priority level 7 case with a threat level of 0 percent. Subject with mental impairment and a loss of the CDG component."

You look around the confined room you're in.

*Priority level 7?*

*Zero percent chance of being a threat?*

*Mental impairment?*

*Loss of the CDG component? Whatever that means.*

"What is CDG again?"

The woman smiles. "That's funny. I do like your humor. It's a lost art, I believe."

"What's going to happen to me?"

"You will be let go. You're obviously not a rebel soldier. We will clean you up and then process you before leaving."

"Cleaning up" means they shave you. *All* of you. Your beard. Your head. *Your body.*

You had more hair when you were born.

You feel naked even after they give you the loose white pants and white shirt to wear. You feel like you're in a kung fu movie.

Then they put you out in the elements—on some crowded street that's dark and rainy and resembles the set of *Blade Runner*.

You have absolutely no idea how to get back to the time machine.

You walk down a couple of blocks, your odd plastic shoes feeling wrong against your bare feet. The raindrops on your bald head make you cold.

As you are about to turn down another street, a figure in a recessed doorway grabs you. Before you strike back at the assailant, you see the glasses.

It's Si.

"Is that you, Willie?"

"Yeah. Of course it is! What are you talking about?"

"It's just been a while since—well, since I've seen your face. And your head."

You have to touch your face before remembering you're as smooth as a newborn baby.

"Quick, we don't have much time," Uncle Si tells you. "We must do something, but you're not going to like it."

You notice Uncle Si is in black-and-gray battle gear, including a black military cap with a red fist logo. He's carrying a gun on his hip and looks tanned and tough.

"What's happened to you? Where have you been, Uncle Si?"

"I'm leading a revolution, man. It's the sixties once again, and I'm John Lennon! I'm just looking for Yoko."

It might be the future, but Uncle Si is still crazy.

"Look, no time to talk," he says. "I gotta open up your skull." He pulls out what appears to be a pen from his belt.

"What is that?" you ask.

"They call it a Split Pea. It opens your skull and takes out the implants they've stuck in your brain."

He presses on it, and two long metal spikes come out of the end, then snap a foot apart.

"And you want to stick that thing . . . in my head?"
"Yes. Right now. Hurry."

**Do you allow Uncle Si to crack open your skull
with the Split Pea? Go to page 183.**

**Do you say no but agree to join Uncle Si,
whatever he's doing? Go to page 121.**

# A LONG, LONG TIME AGO

WHEN THE MACHINE touches down with a jolt, you step out and feel the hot sun beating down on you. At least you know John Luke, Jase, and Si weren't pranking you. The question now is where the time machine brought you and whether your family members are around here somewhere too. This must be a faraway place. It doesn't look anything like West Monroe. Or even like America, for that matter.

You call out for Phil several times, but he's not around. For all you know, he could be in a totally different year. You couldn't find a time machine instruction manual inside and had no idea how to direct the machine.

You appear to be in a desert of some kind, walking on a dirt road that looks frequently traveled, but not by cars.

You only see footprints and animal prints, from horses and other creatures you can't determine.

Maybe this is a different continent or something.

Just then, a figure in a long black robe approaches you. He's wearing a hood, and you wonder if it's Phil. But when he pulls off the hood, you recognize him instantly.

"Hey, aren't you O—?"

"Oh no, you don't," the old man with white hair and a beard says. "We don't want to cause any issues."

It's totally him. Or someone who looks like him.

"What issues?" you ask.

"Licensing issues."

You shake your head, not understanding. "Am I on a movie set?"

"No. Please. Listen to me now. You were meant to meet someone in the time machine, someone who would have explained the most important element of time travel—the level 34-B bicode. But he didn't arrive on schedule, so you have no way of knowing." The man takes a deep breath. "The bicode ensures that you can't die in other places and times. Anything can happen . . . but if you die, you'll just find yourself back where you started."

"Oh . . . uh, that's great." But you don't plan to die anytime soon, for fake or for real. You glance around and finally get where you are. "Is this the planet of Tat—?"

"Ah, ah, ah," he interrupts. "Please. You must choose right this instant. Will you go back to your time machine or won't you?"

You consider it for a minute.

"What is your decision?"

"Will you give me the page numbers?" you ask.

He nods.

**If you choose to go back to the time machine, turn to page 197.**

**And if you decide to stay out here where something bad is obviously going to happen, go to page 95.**

"That's certainly a difficult choice."

# 2319

HOW CAN YOU *NOT* STAY and help Si fight this war?
Maybe you'll be gone for a few weeks, maybe longer. But
this is for a noble cause. People's lives are in danger. The
future is in your hands.

A week into the war, you lose your left arm. Yes, this is
a horrible thing. But it's the future, so they simply give you
a new arm. And the cool thing is that this arm is stronger
and better than your old one. It can pulverize rocks while
at the same time allowing you to watch a movie on your
palm.

This is the start of the fog.

The fog begins to seep inside your thoughts.

Every now and then, you have dreams or nightmares of

circuitry and wiring and computer data. You hear strange computerized voices that remind you of Siri. You don't feel so right with your body.

Perhaps it's being in the future. Perhaps it's your synthetic arm.

Then you lose your leg in battle and the same thing happens.

Then you lose an ear and they give you a new one.

Little by little, you start becoming one of them. A machine.

And little by little, the person you once were goes away.

The day comes when you win the war. But it's been years. Uncle Si has been in an institution ever since losing the Tupperware cups his mother sent him when he was in Vietnam. You've forgotten where you're from and how you got here. You don't feel like yourself at all. And that's because half of you really isn't you.

You live out the rest of your life in the future. Cyborg Willie: half machine.

And then, one day, when you finally take your last breath—and you utter a barely heard quack before dying—you're blasted into the past.

You find yourself back in West Monroe, back in the present day, back as your former self, back at Duck Commander.

And when the Britney Spears ringtone comes on, you've never been more joyful to hear that sweet, precious, beautiful song—"Oops! . . . I Did It Again." 'Cause it means you're back. And all your body parts are *your* parts.

## THE END

# 1990

**YES, YOU SHOULD BE LOOKING** for John Luke in order
to get out of here.

Yes, they've started playing "Girl You Know It's True" by
Milli Vanilli, and you really feel like dancing just a little bit.
A girl jumps up and down right next to you, saying how
much she loves this song.

"They're not really the ones who sing it," you tell her.
"Just so you know."

She has no idea what you're talking about. No big deal.

You wonder if the time machine that brought you here
is still in the hallway.

But you know you have to do this. There's no way you
can't.

You see one of the football players you used to be on the
team with. Jack is a senior who played wide receiver. He's

a good guy, and you can't remember who he took to prom. But it doesn't matter.

You remember who he ends up marrying.

"Jack," you call out above the music. "How ya doin'?"

The guy looks perplexed that you're talking to him.

"You want to earn a hundred bucks?"

A hundred dollars is good money, but back in 1990 it was quite a bit of cash.

"Sure."

"I want you to dance with Samantha Price."

A lot of guys would say no, but you remember Jack as someone who turns out to be a very good businessman. He's also not a very prideful guy, which helps in a situation like this.

"You want me to dance with Samantha?"

"Yeah. For a hundred bucks."

"Thought she was dating Rick," he says.

"Rick broke up with her."

"How do you know all this?" Jack asks.

Yeah, it does seem sorta weird, this older dude nobody recognizes who knows all these details about the students.

"I'm a friend of the family."

"*What* family?"

"Just a family. Will you do it or not?"

Jack looks at the dance floor, then glances at Samantha. "Okay. I guess."

"First slow song."

"My date isn't going to like it."

"Split the money with her," you say. "Go spend it on her."

"Samantha might not even want to dance. She's always liked Rick."

"Just because someone's attached to another's hip doesn't mean they'll end up with that person," you tell him.

Jack looks at you but doesn't get it. But that's okay. You put the money in his hand.

"First slow song."

A slow song that sounds like cotton candy begins to play, and you see Jack asking Samantha for a dance. At first she doesn't agree and looks embarrassed, but he talks to her a bit and says something that makes her nod. Soon they're out on the floor.

You watch them and see an actual smile come over Samantha's face. You're not sure if you ever saw it before. Not even once when she was with jerk-boy Rick.

It's a nice thing to witness.

You know it'll be something she never forgets. You'll always remember the best and worst parts about high school. They stick with you like diamonds on a finger or gum in your hair.

She'll also always remember the first time she danced with the man she ended up marrying and spending the rest of her life with.

The song is nearly over when you look out at the dancing couples and spot Korie again. She's dancing with someone who looks a lot like you. . . .

*Wait a minute—that's not 1990 me.*

It's John Luke.

John Luke and his mullet.

Somehow he's got a tuxedo on.

And now he's dancing with his mother.

This is a total *Back to the Future* moment.

You pause, watching them, unsure what exactly to do.

**Do you watch your wife and your son dance
in a fond sort of weird, wonderful way?
Go to page 113.**


**Do you decide to interrupt them and break
up this moment? Go to page 109.**

# 2319

SI STARTS PUSHING BUTTONS and pulls down a lever, then another. Soon you guys are moving, and the machine seems to be alive again.

Where you're headed . . . well, that's a good question.

The vibration lasts only for a minute; then everything is still again.

"What'd you press?" you shout.

"Anything I could."

You sigh in frustration. If you could actually learn how to operate the time machine, maybe you and Si could get home instead of traveling to random corners of the space-time continuum.

Sirens go off, and the word *Danger* flashes on multiple screens around you.

"Did you press a Danger button?" you shout.

"Man, I'm like Michael Dangerous. I'm dangerous."

"You're something," you tell Si. "Tell me this. Why does the door open sometimes, but other times it doesn't?"

"You think I know? It's not my fault. This isn't some elevator with a Door Open button."

"I knew it was trouble."

Right then the door to the machine opens.

"So what do you think our odds will be?" Si asks.

The first thing you see is a fire. Not just a small fire but a big, blazing one. You see people screaming and running away from what looks like a big fair. A Ferris wheel is crumbling. Booths are crackling. A group of panicked clowns sprints past you.

"Hey," you shout to one, grabbing and stopping him. "What happened?"

"Something landed on a Ford Model T that was next to a gas supply, and the whole thing exploded."

You shake your head. "Next to a gas supply? That seems a bit—"

But the clown can't take any more, especially since his makeup is running down his face from the heat.

You and Si look at the chaos caused when your time machine landed in the wrong place.

What you don't know is that you've set off a cataclysmic chain reaction.

This happens to be the 1919 Texas state fair. If you hadn't destroyed it, this would have been the first place snow cones were ever served. They would have been made by Samuel Bert of Dallas. He would have gone on to make the first snow cone machine a year later—if this tragic fire hadn't destroyed his little stand and stopped him from serving the cold treat to kids everywhere.

You have deprived the world of its favorite summer snack.

The world has become a darker place.

Your actions send humanity into a downward spiral where kids who would have normally grown up eating strawberry-flavored snow cones are now forced to eat average, boring candy. Watermelon snow cones and peach snow cones and blueberry snow cones never see the light of day.

In their place come criminals and angry, depressed people.

All because of your little mishap.

You want a Reset button.

You want to do it all over again and give the world back its snow cones.

## THE END

# 1990

YOU GRAB JOHN LUKE by the arm and sprint to the gym doors as you hear the beginning of the OMD song "If You Leave."

The two of you head into the hallway, and you start to go in one direction until John Luke tells you to turn the other way. You follow John Luke, and there's the outhouse, just waiting for you guys.

"Can't believe it's still here," you say as you open the door.

Just like the first time John Luke opened it, the inside resembles that of a typical outhouse. You have to move and squeeze so both of you can fit.

"Well, let's see what happens," you say as you shut the door.

For a second the two of you stand in silent darkness.

"Think it's the wrong outhouse?" John Luke asks.

Then, finally, everything changes. You're standing in the control room of the time machine. You sigh in relief.

"Do you know how to operate this thing?" you ask John Luke. Although, considering the way he drives cars, you're a little afraid to even ask.

"I was just pressing buttons on the screen and the thing took off."

"We need to go back to the present day," you say.

John Luke stands in front of one of the control panels. He runs a finger across the buttons before saying, "Found it," then types something on a keyboard.

"What'd you find?"

"A place to put dates in."

He enters the date, then presses a sequence of buttons.

The time machine springs to life with a loud rumbling. You feel like you're riding on a roller coaster.

"Where are we going to land?" you ask.

John Luke just shrugs.

"Did it give a time?"

"I didn't put one."

"Maybe you should have—"

Suddenly you're falling sideways against the wall next to you. John Luke crashes into you. Then you're both on the floor. The whirring stops, and the door opens.

You're afraid to go outside but know you have to. John

Luke is about to go first, but this time you hold him back, stepping through the doorway ahead of him.

You discover you're in a field.

*The field behind our house!*

It looks like it's later in the day than when you left, since the sun is disappearing. John Luke comes out and stands beside you.

"Dad, look!"

John Luke points to the sky and you see it. Someone's coming toward you, parachuting down. He's swinging back and forth and seems to be having a difficult time adjusting his position. The closer he gets, the more the person looks like . . .

"Is that Uncle Si?" John Luke asks.

You nod.

What in the world is Uncle Si doing parachuting from the sky?

**Do you stay and wait for Uncle Si to land safely?
Go to page 193.**

**Do you get inside to make sure you have
a gift for Korie's party, which should be
starting any minute now? Go to page 247.**

# 2319

YOU SMILE AT THE WOMAN interrogating you.

"I'm wondering—have you seen Chewbacca anywhere? Maybe Luke?"

She doesn't smile.

In fact, your remark seems to have made her very unhappy.

She pulls out a round, disklike thing and places it in the palm of her hand. It begins to hover.

"That's cool," you tell her, trying to show that you're a friendly, good guy.

You can see she's reading something on the disk.

"I think, Willie Jess Robertson, born April 22, 1972, it's definitely not 'cool.'"

"Wow—future technology. Did you buy that at Radio-Shack?"

She lets out a fake laugh as she grabs the disk and turns it toward you. You see a screen like a small, round television. On it is an image of your face.

*What is that?*

"That is you," she says.

*You can read minds?*

"Yours I can. Good-bye, Mr. Robertson."

You wake up and find that you're a construction worker in the year 1990. It's strange because you end up having these confusing memories. Of West Monroe. Of going to the future. Of having a beard. Even of Mars.

But, alas, you spend the rest of your life beardless and West Monroe–less and never even know what a duck call really is.

Until, of course, someone suggests you get a memory implant, an amazing new procedure that will allow you to experience a fully imagined other life.

This gives you déjà vu, but you really can't recall why.

## THE END

# TODAY

"WELL, LOOKY WHAT WE GOT HERE," a voice says from across the warehouse.

You're sitting on a box of Duck Commander hats in front of the mystery outhouse as Phil strides over. He's wearing all camo and has shades on. He stands right next to you, staring at the outhouse.

"Go ahead, get inside," you tell him.

"Why so glum?"

You doubt your father is involved with the joke everyone else seems to be playing. But then again, maybe *everybody's* in on it.

"You know why this thing's here?" you ask.

"No, sirree," Phil says. "What would I know about a wooden shed containing a toilet in the middle of your warehouse?"

"I don't know. People keep getting inside and then disappearing."

Phil looks at you and nods slowly. He examines the control panel on the door.

"I bet you're going to get inside and disappear too, right?" you say.

"A man doesn't go into an outhouse unless he's got business to take care of," Phil says in his trademark quotable tone.

"You seen John Luke, Jase, or Si?" you ask.

"They're all in there?"

You smile. Maybe Phil is indeed a part of this. "Oh yeah. They all went in, but they didn't come out. It's one of *those* outhouses."

"Sounds like the Mafia to me." Phil opens the door and looks inside. "Ain't smelling anything, so that's a good thing," he says.

"Ain't seeing anybody, so that's a strange thing," you reply.

"So if I go inside and come right out, will you take me to get some lunch?" Phil asks.

"I'll even *pay*," you say.

"Okay. I'm hungry. That's all I gotta say."

The tall, lean figure of Phil steps into the outhouse. The door swings shut, and the lights flash blue and green. You knew this would happen—maybe Phil will pay for your lunch instead. If you ever find him, that is. You'd hear

something if your family members were all escaping into a secret underground tunnel or through a back door.

The lights blink one more time, and the door opens.

"I bet you're not there, are you?" you say.

You look around the warehouse to see if someone's *finally* going to jump out and surprise you. But, nope. So you check the outhouse again.

Empty.

Unoccupied.

Abandoned.

Deserted.

You stand there and think for a minute.

Some say you can be stubborn, but they're wrong—what you really are is smart. Caution can be an asset. And sometimes being suspicious can save you time and money.

Plus, you have two older brothers and a younger one, and also five kids. You know the importance of being careful about what's behind the door. *Lots* of things have been behind doors in the Robertson home.

But now that Phil has vanished—and you know he's not much into playing pranks—you think that something really, truly might be going on with this outhouse.

Sometimes it pays to hold back, but sometimes you simply gotta get on with it.

You step inside the wooden box and shut the door behind

you. It doesn't take long to realize that you were wrong, for what you're standing in is not an outhouse anymore.

**Do you press a flashing button on a control panel in front of you? Go to page 157.**

**Do you decide you better not touch anything until you can figure out what's going on? Go to page 15.**

# 2319

**YOU JUST LET UNCLE SI** crack open your head to find a hidden implant in your brain.

Are you crazy?

Has the time travel really gotten to you?

When Si tries to do whatever he needs to do to your head, something seems to go wrong, and he falls back a moment.

"What? What is it?"

You're feeling a bit woozy.

"What happened?" you ask.

"Are you—? You can still talk?"

"Yeah."

You try to put your hand on your head. But then you realize you're missing a big chunk of it.

"That can't be good," you say.

Si just stammers, "I-I thought I knew how to work one of these things."

"And you tell me that—" *Now?*

Those are the last words you will ever say.

Until you hear a familiar song and find yourself singing along. "Yeah, yeah, yeah, yeah, yeah, yeah."

Your phone is ringing. Somehow you're back in your warehouse. And somehow . . .

Wait a minute. Where are you back from?

And why's your head pounding?

## THE END

# 2038

YOU REALIZE YOU DON'T *WANT* to see the future. It's too weird. This store and John Luke and that little car. Thanks but no thanks. You can experience 2038 after living another twenty-odd years, as you explain to John Luke before you go back through the Walmazon doors.

Wandering down an aisle, you try to find the men's restroom. Surely the outhouse will still be there, right?

You pass a huge display that shows guys wearing some kind of strange camouflage you've never seen before. Then you read the header.

**Squirrel & Girls**

There are T-shirts and toys and books and even Chia Pets. *Wait a minute.*

Everything looks like Duck Commander. They even have a logo of . . . a squirrel.

*What is this?*

You go over to a lady behind the jewelry counter.

"Hey, what's this Squirrel & Girls?"

"Oh, they're great."

"Who are they?"

"A family living in Monronia."

You lean over because you think you didn't hear her right. "Mon*ronia*? What's that?"

"Our town. You from out of town?"

*Yeah, I'm from out of this world.* "Something like that," you say. "So what do they do?"

"Oh, they're great. Funny. It's a mother and father—the mom used to hunt squirrels, and now the four daughters all do the same. They're a huge brand. They sell everything. They've had four movies come out. You didn't see them?"

"Movies?"

"Sure," the woman says. "I watched one on my refrigerator the other morning. It was good."

Somehow it seems like every other word this lady is saying isn't coming out right.

"What's the movie called?"

"Oh, *The Dark Squirrel Rises.*"

This must be the bizarro future caused by something you ate. Again you remember those fried pickles from right before you got into the machine.

"Okay, thanks."

"But don't start there," the woman says as you begin to leave. "Start with *Star Squirrels*. Then *The Squirrel Who Loved Me*."

"Will do."

You gotta get out of here.

Before you leave the Squirrel & Girls merchandise center, you see a stack of boxes that say *Chia Jillie*. You can only shake your head and keep going.

When you get to the restroom, you see workmen carrying pieces of wood out of it. You rush in and find what remains of the time machine: a pile of scraps.

It's been battered and destroyed.

You're never going back home, back to 2014.

You decide to shout a loud and long "noooooooooo!"

"Greetings, Willie," a voice behind you says.

But you're still yelling, "Noooooooooo!"

Eventually you stop.

"Willie Robertson. The once-famous Duckman."

You look up and see an older guy staring at you. The workmen leave the scraps so you two can have a private conversation.

"Do I know you?" you ask the older man, who, strangely enough, sorta looks like you.

He's got a thick gray beard and long hair and even has a bandanna on his head.

"It's Henry Billowby. From West Monroe High."

Of all the people you could imagine meeting right here and now, he never would have crossed your mind.

"And yes, I know you're probably wondering what I'm doing here."

"I'm wondering what *I'm* doing here," you say.

"Since I'm really the only villain your story has, of course I need to show up at some point. Don't you think?"

"I'm not quite following."

"The world has changed, Willie. Duckman. Ever since you decided to come back and pick a fight with my brother and me when you saw us in high school. Remember?"

"That never—"

"Oh yes, it did," he interrupts. "And it changed the course of everything. Everything."

You stare at the busted time machine.

"What'd you do?" you ask.

"For one thing, I helped get legislation in place to make duck hunting illegal."

"You what?"

Henry nods. He looks seriously sorta crazy.

"That's right. No more duck hunting. Ever. And you know what happened then? That meant no more Duck Commander. It opened up room for my franchise."

"Let me guess . . . Squirrel & Girls."

"Yes. And we're bigger than anything Duck Commander did. We have our own movies. That's right. Full length. With special effects. Forget books about time travel. We filmed scenes with space travel."

"I'm getting out of here," you say.

"Oh no."

Now he's pointing a mysterious object at you. Something that resembles a lollipop.

"This is a blowgun. The round top contains a synthetic blast that could kill you instantly."

You laugh. "This is ridiculous."

"I mean it!" he screams. "Now I order you to get into the second stall over there."

"What for?"

"You'll see."

"Look, Henry, whatever you might—"

"Now!" he screams as he waves the lollipop-like thing at your head.

"Okay, fine."

You start to enter one of the bathroom stalls.

"The second one!"

You step inside and wait.

"Can I come out?"

You keep waiting. You don't hear anything.

"Henry?"

You decide to slowly open the door.

When you do, blue skies surround you, with similarly colored water below. You see hills in every direction.

Then you spot a field of ducks. Hundreds, maybe thousands of ducks.

You don't know this now, but you're in a place called Kendahari, which is a small town in Malaysia. Five people live here. Now there are six.

You never learn the year because you can't speak the language. All you know is that this place protects ducks. They love ducks. They're pets.

Here in Kendahari, you have to live alongside ducks for the rest of your life. And you can never harm them nor eat them nor anger them.

You will forever be haunted by ducks. Thanks to Henry Billowby and your time travel machine.

You knew you shouldn't have gone inside it.

You find yourself wishing you could go back, right to the moment before you spotted the time machine, when you were innocent and busy and didn't even know time travel was possible.

Funny thing about wishes, however.

Sometimes they come true.

## THE END

# TODAY

YOU AND JOHN LUKE watch as Si attempts to guide his parachute down toward your backyard. He does a terrible job and ends up stuck in a tree. You send John Luke up there to cut him down.

Once Si has his feet back on earth, you ask him what's going on. He's got some kind of weird astronaut outfit on.

"There's been a space-time continuum problem," Si says. "You have to go back to the future."

You and John Luke stare at each other.

"Si, what are you talking about?"

"You want to know what I'm talking about? Look, I'm tired. I just survived an alien in my spaceship, a computer taking over my craft, a flight around the moon, and destroying the evil Dismal One. And that's all *before* I learned the future of the world *depends* on you getting in that time machine and setting it to the year 2319."

Si's not the only one who is tired. "Look, Si, seriously— I don't think we should use that time machine again anytime soon. I barely managed to get John Luke back."

He yanks the front of your shirt and pulls you to him. His eyes get big behind his glasses.

"It's the fate of all mankind in your hands. *The fate of the world.*"

"Dad—it's the fate of all mankind."

"Be quiet, John Luke," you say.

You see Jep and his family entering your house for Korie's birthday party.

You *really* don't want to get back in that time machine.

**Do you decide to go to the party and ignore Si's warning? Turn to page 231.**

**Do you get in the time machine by yourself and set it for the year 2319? Go to page 71.**

# A LONG, LONG
# TIME AGO

YOU RETURN TO THE TIME MACHINE and end up face-to-face with the old guy in the robe again.

"Good choice," he says.

"Am I supposed to leave?"

"You can't leave. You must go out and fulfill your mission."

"My mission?"

He nods. "Yes. To go and build the great bridge over the River Kwai." Then he stops for a moment. "No, no, I'm sorry. That is not this story."

You're very confused now. "Do you know where my son is? Or my brother? Or my uncle? Or my father?"

"Did your whole family get lost?" he asks—or jokes. You can't tell which is which with him.

"Seems that way."

"You, my big bearded brother, are going to head out there into the brave unknown."

You point to the open door. "You mean the place I just came from? The place where I met you?"

"Yes, yes. Just—it sounds better that way."

"Okay."

The old man presses a button on the wall. Underneath it, a panel drops open, revealing a table with three different items on it. "One of these things will help you in your journey." He picks up the first one. "You have a personal flotation device right here."

"That's a life jacket," you say.

"It's a personal flotation device. The second is a distress pull cord."

You shake your head. "A what? That's like Batman's gun. It's a grappling-hook gun."

He chooses to ignore you. "The third is a chainsaw."

"Oh, you're not going to call it a metal teeth-cruncher thing?" you joke.

The old man doesn't laugh.

It's time to choose.

"So either I have to float on water somewhere, climb up a castle, or cut down a tree?"

His expression doesn't change. "Choose, and choose now."

**Do you pick the life jacket?**

**Go to page 75.**

**Do you pick the grappling-hook gun?**

**Go to page 215.**

**Do you pick the chainsaw?**

**Go to page 117.**

# 2038

SO YOU DECIDE TO GET IN THE CAR with John Luke (which requires a little bit of time since the car is both low and tiny) and allow him to drive away. You look at him while you're coasting through a parking lot.

"This is really weird," you say.

"I understand."

His voice sounds so . . . adult.

"What are you doing now?" you ask him.

"I'm a professor teaching at Louisiana State."

You can't help but laugh. "How'd *that* happen?"

"I went to college and studied and became a professor."

"And what about the family business?"

John Luke shakes his head. "There is no more business. You and Mom decided to open a fitness and yoga place."

"What?"

He doesn't look like he's joking. He turns and gets on a road that resembles I-20. But it's different because the road seems to vanish ahead.

"All interstates are underground now," John Luke says as you enter a tunnel. "They need less maintenance, and it helps with all the pollution."

"Okay. What's the yoga place called?"

"Body by WillKore."

Something is definitely wrong with this future. You're just not sure why.

"Uh, Professor John Luke? Are you married?"

"Yep."

"Kids?"

"Have three of them."

"How did you meet your wife?" you ask.

"Remember the thing—well, of course you remember it. Twitter? I actually found this girl who was a super-big fan of mine on Twitter. She turned out to be a sweet girl who loves the Lord and is a wonderful soul."

"You found her on Twitter?"

He nods.

Again, you know something is really not right with the universe.

The car enters sunlight again.

"Are we heading back home?"

"Oh no. I can't do that to you. I'm driving back to the other machine. To set things right."

Some of the scenery looks exactly the same as it did—well, back in the present. Then you're underground on another highway.

"Tell me about the rest of the family," you say, curious but almost afraid to ask.

"Let's see," John Luke says, clearing his throat. "Jase became a professional golfer."

"What?"

"Yes. Won the Masters *twice*. Uncle Al took his family and moved to New York City to start up a ministry. It's currently the only active church in the city. And Uncle Jep . . . he's doing his thing."

"What happened?"

"He, uh—after he went on *Dancing with the Stars*, the whole music thing opened up for him. He's got some of the bestselling albums of all time now."

You start laughing and almost can't stop. This is all pure insanity.

*The fried pickles went to my head.*

"What sort of albums did he do?"

"Disco. Which, well, you know. Disco went out in the seventies. But actually it came back about five years ago—when Jep brought it back. The album you and Jase sang on with him was the biggest seller. You were like the Bee Gees, except—well, you're the J-Robs."

Before you can ask about the rest of the family, John Luke exits the new underground highway thing and heads down a country road.

"Taking me to another outhouse?" you ask John Luke.

He shakes his head. "No. But I am taking you to another time machine."

You look at his goatee. "You finally grew some facial hair, huh?"

"Yes. But my wife wanted me to keep the dimple showing. It was a big campaign on Twitter—#keepthedimple." John Luke doesn't laugh like he thinks this is funny or ridiculous.

"Whatever happened to Twitter?"

He sighs. "There was like a whole war and everything. It got ugly."

"A war. Like a media war or something?"

"No. Like a literal war. Anyway, long story. There's not enough time."

He slows down at a small, winding street off the dirt road you're on. Then he turns and drives for about five minutes before arriving at an old wooden barn.

"Is that the time machine?" you ask.

"No. They can't get them *that* big."

"So, John Luke." You have to ask before leaving this weird and wacky world. "Are you happy? Now? In your life?"

He nods. "Yeah. Got a great family. God has been good to us. Can't complain."

This is good to hear. Despite all the strangeness.

You both walk into the barn, and after the lights go on, you discover the driver's seat from a car.

"You just sit down there and it transports you to wherever you think of going," John Luke says.

For a moment you consider all the places you'd like to go. But then you realize you have to go back to the moment you made the mistake of deciding to get the po'boy sandwich at Duck Diner.

"Anywhere I want to go? I just have to think about it?"

John Luke nods. You can't help noticing how tall he is now.

"Man, you really grew, didn't you?" you say.

"It's funny seeing you in a beard, Dad. You haven't had one in years."

"I don't think I was meant to be a yoga instructor," you say.

"I don't either. A lot of things have seemed weird. I think—I don't know. I think you might be able to help by going back in time."

You look at the car seat and think you recognize it.

"Is that from your Jeep?"

John Luke nods. "Yep. I kept it for nostalgia."

"Or did you eventually crash it, and that was the only piece left?"

"Well . . ."

You give your son a hug and decide to get in the driver's seat. But one thing before you leave.

"Okay, I just gotta ask—" you begin to say.

"Sadie started an orphanage in the Dominican Republic. Rebecca's fashion line is now worldwide. Will is a big-time music producer who helped with Jep's albums. And Bella is a famous chef. She cooks for a restaurant on Mars."

You nod. "These all seem totally believable."

With a smile and a handshake for John Luke, you take a seat. You focus on the moment you chose to go to Duck Diner instead of getting in the outhouse right away, and the driver's seat begins to spin.

Maybe you're not ready to face this future just yet.

## THE END

# 1990

YOU HAVE THIS CRAZY IDEA. So crazy it's going to be crazy awesome.

You're going to give these students something they'll never forget. They won't be ready for it. It'll be like they get hit by a tsunami of groovy love.

You head for the DJ at the back of the gym. "Hey, buddy. I'm wondering if I can play a song."

The DJ looks sleepy-eyed and pretty laid-back. You could probably ask him anything and he'd say, *"Yeah, sure, whatever."*

You pull your iPhone out of your pocket and try to see if the DJ has anything to hook it up with.

But it's 1990, and things weren't so simple back then. You can't just find a plug-in and play music from your phone.

"What's that thing?" the DJ asks.

"This? It's my phone."

The guy shrugs. He seems quite out of it.

"I'm from the future," you tell him.

"Me too," he says.

You laugh. Then he pulls out something that resembles a Post-it note. He turns it on with a tap.

"What is that?"

"My communicator. Phones eventually go obsolete." The hippie-looking dude is not smiling.

"Are you for real?" you ask him.

"Are you?"

"So would you be able to hook my phone up so I could play a song?"

The DJ just nods.

*Cool.* "Okay, here. This is the song I want to play."

The DJ looks at your phone. "Whoa. I don't know, man."

"What?"

"I don't know if the world is ready for this."

"They better be ready, 'cause I'm gonna bring the boom."

Hippie DJ just stares at you. He obviously doesn't get your joke. Whatever.

When the music stops, you go to the middle of the floor carrying a microphone the DJ gave you.

"Good evening, everyone. How's everybody doing?"

Nobody says a word. They're all looking at you, wondering why the music is off, wondering who in the world you are.

"Listen, Principal Zachary told me I could introduce a song to you." You use the principal's name 'cause you know for a fact he's not here. You remember he skipped this prom when he got sick right beforehand, but no one realized this until afterward. You figured you better mention his name so one of the teachers or chaperones doesn't escort you out of here. "But I'm gonna need some help. You guys interested in learning a dance?"

Two kids say yes, but the rest of the room is quiet.

"Okay, come on—I swear you're gonna love this song." You peer into the cluster of students. "Is John Luke in the building? John Luke, you here?"

You see John Luke come out of the crowd.

"You gotta help me, okay?" you whisper to him.

"Help you do what? We gotta get out of here."

You return the mike to your mouth. "Okay, boys and girls. I'm going to introduce you to a song you're gonna love."

You motion for Hippie DJ to start the music. The zany electronic beat begins.

"'Oppa Gangnam Style,'" Psy starts to sing. The stream of Korean lyrics continues. You can tell everybody in the room is completely perplexed and wondering what's going on. They've obviously never heard K-pop—Korean pop—before.

"Here you go. Watch me now," you shout as you start doing the moves.

For the first minute, nobody is dancing. But you and John Luke keep showing everybody how it's done, and a few brave souls start trying. Then more. Then you have a whole wave of kids trying out the motions. John Luke rejoins the crowd as the steps catch on.

"Come on; let's go!" you shout as the chorus nears and the signature moves begin.

You make the motions of riding a horse. Soon the whole room is doing the same thing.

"You're getting it. That's right."

You glance toward John Luke and see Korie dancing at his side. Dancing as if she knows him.

*Uh-oh.*

John Luke is staring at you like, *Dad, let's get out of here.*

You just laugh and make the lasso motion again.

As the song nears its end, you decide to get a little fancy with your footwork, hoping to move around John Luke and Korie. But your boots get tangled and you trip and fall.

You don't just fall. You fall *hard*.

Hard enough to black out.

• • •

When you awake, you're in a hospital bed. You can feel the bandages on your head and the IV in your arm. You feel woozy, and all you can hear are the whirring sounds of "Gangnam Style." The door opens, and you expect John Luke to enter the room. Maybe he'll be able to help you get out of here. But instead a man in a black suit comes in and shuts the door behind him. He comes and sits right by you.

"How are you feeling, Mr. Robertson?"

"Fine," you say. "And it's Willie."

"Having fun at high school proms?" the man in the suit asks.

He's maybe in his thirties and has sharp, cutting eyes that don't wander.

"Yeah, it was a good time."

"You do know there are penalties for doing what you did tonight."

You don't quite understand him. "Penalties? What do you mean? For hitting my head?"

"For sharing music the way you did."

This guy is coming down on you for file sharing?

"What are you talking about? All I did was play a song—"

"The world is not supposed to hear 'Gangnam Style.'"

You laugh. "Uh-oh. Did I tilt the earth's axis by playing it too soon? What are you, the pop music police?"

The man reaches into his suit coat and pulls out his wallet. He opens it to reveal his badge. "My name is Conan Skywalker Rambo. Of course, that's not my real name."

"Oh, really?" you ask without any humor.

You just want to get out of here and stop talking to this guy.

"I'm Member 004 of the PCP."

"A secret agent?" you ask.

"It's called the Pop Culture Police. We monitor the well-being and structure of pop culture, and have done so since the 1960s."

This guy is acting serious, as if this isn't some big joke.

"Are you for real?"

He nods.

"So what'd I do?"

"The timing of 'Gangnam Style' is critical to the *plan* we have for the music industry. It can't be heard until 2012. And as you know, that's twenty-two years from now. These kids are still fine with their Bell Biv DeVoe and their Jon Bon Jovi."

"So do you give me a pop culture fine? Like I have to do an overnight listening to Poison or something?"

You're trying to make a joke, but this man doesn't think it's funny.

"We have a list of the ten songs you most hate with a passion," the man says. "You will be forced to listen to these for one week straight."

"Are you serious? You're crazy, right?"

He shakes his head. "No. I'm sorry, but the balance of culture must be maintained. We now have to erase the memory of 'Gangnam Style' from the mind of every single student who was in that gym tonight."

"How do you do that?"

"We have our ways. We might show them four of the worst movies ever made back-to-back-to-back-to-back. Or we might let them hear or see pieces of music or songs that have been held in the vault."

"Held in the vault," you repeat. "Why?"

"That is not for you to know, Willie. Now I'm sorry, but here you go."

He hands you an iPod with headphones.

Then he points a gun at you. "Put those on now."

• • •

You make it only a day before you go certifiably insane.

You're stuck forever humming the tunes of the songs you hate the most.

Over.

And over.

And over again.

Until a track comes on, and . . .

And everything changes.

Sure, you don't like this song, but it also seems to spark something different in your mind.

In fact, you realize you're no longer listening to the iPod. You're back in your warehouse.

The Pop Culture Police might have tried to kill you, but the time travel lords have overruled them.

Oops.

## THE END

# A LONG, LONG
# TIME AGO

YOU BEGIN TO WALK DOWN the worn-out road in front of the time machine, grappling hook in hand. Rain begins to fall, and soon you're soaked. Your jeans stick to your legs more tightly the wetter they get. And a guy in skinny jeans is just not a good thing. It will never be a good thing.

You encounter a woman who looks like she's planning to cross the road. But she catches sight of you and the thing you're carrying and bolts the other way. From the way she's dressed, you realize you must be in the olden days. Like the really olden days. Biblical times or something.

You keep heading along the road until you reach a small village. It reminds you of the place Frodo and Bilbo live in those Lord of the Rings movies. The Shire. That's it. This is the Shire, except it looks like these set designers were fourth graders.

Nobody is outdoors, and if anyone's inside the huts, they won't open their crudely made doors when you knock. Impatient, you finally just open one, and the woman inside screams.

"I'm not going to hurt anybody," you tell her.

"Please, my child."

Good news is, they speak the same language here.

*Or maybe I speak the same language they do.*

"What's the name of this place?"

The woman shakes her head like she doesn't know what you're talking about.

"The year? The closest town?"

"Are you with the one who built the boat?"

You hear thunder and wipe your dripping face. Your shirt and jeans are soaked.

"Uh, the one who built the boat?" you ask, curious about that. "What's his name?"

"Noah."

You look around the dark, enclosed hut.

*There's no way.*

Of course, your mind's been saying that ever since you set foot in the time machine. But now . . . Could you really be here? All the way back in Noah's time?

"Did Noah build this boat?"

The woman nods. "He said God would wipe out the world with a flood."

Thunder sounds again.

You aren't that thrilled to be back in Noah's time. And you totally don't know how you're going to use this grappling hook.

*Why in the world do I have a weapon Batman would use? A grappling-hook gun?*

"Where is this Noah?" you ask.

The woman tells you where the boat is located. So far she's never said the word *ark*, but you have an idea that this boat will turn out to be it.

It takes you about an hour to reach the vessel. And the sight of it blows you away.

The ark looks far bigger than you've ever imagined or even seen in drawings or films. It's more square than rectangular too. It's like a massive box made of wood. You can't see any windows or doors or anything.

The rain continues to fall, and as you approach the ark, you see people huddled around it. Some simply look on; some shout; some throw things.

This is no longer a nice little bedtime story or a Sunday school tale. This is real.

It's real and somewhat scary.

You avoid the group of people and circle to the other side of the ark, trying to see if there's any way in.

The boat seems to be made up of layers, much the way a pyramid might be built. From what you can tell, the ark is about three layers tall.

You think about the options you were allowed to choose from before leaving the time machine. Now they make sense. Especially the grappling hook you're carrying.

You find a place where nobody can see you. Then you fire the gun, trying to get the grappling hook over the square edge of the ark. It doesn't work, so you have to try again.

It takes you five tries.

Once the grappling hook is secure, you begin to climb the rope. It's wet and a bit slippery, but you realize you're climbing for your life. Maybe your father's life. Maybe others'.

The climbing is . . . well, let's say it's been a while since you climbed up a sheer wooden wall using only a rope. Or maybe you never have. As you struggle, making a little progress, then hanging on and just breathing in and out, you come to regret the elk meat you had for breakfast.

As you make it to the ledge, you hear screams and cries from the people below. They've spotted you. You quickly pull up the rope. You don't want to change history—you simply want to find Phil and get out of here. Maybe check out a few animals on the ark. But that's all.

You circle the ledge you're on, looking for some kind of entrance. Soon you spot one near the front of the ark. It's a round opening big enough to put your hand into. Rainwater can't get in because of the hole's angle. You put your entire arm through and manage to pull open a door concealed in the wall.

You slip inside to darkness.

**Do you search the deck you're on?**
**Go to page 21.**


**Do you stay put until you hear voices?**
**Go to page 37.**

# 2319

YOU DECIDE TO TELL THE WOMAN in the military outfit everything. Who you are and where you're from and how you got here. She seems most curious about the time machine.

"You say it resembles an outhouse?" she asks. "What would that be?"

"It's sorta like—well, it's usually something outdoors where you can go take a break. You know—use the bathroom."

She nods. "I see. A Vitronic Controllock."

"Is that—? You're referring to the outhouse?"

"It's interesting that you've managed to get here that way. And you say this man who came before you . . . his name is Si?"

"Yes."

She goes to the wall in front of you and touches it. Immediately a photo of Si's face appears on the wall.

"Is this the man you're referring to?"

You nod.

"Thank you for your honesty."

The picture of Si goes away.

"So can you let me go?" you ask, looking down at your hands, which still can't move.

"That is one thing we can't do."

The door opens and three men dressed all in black step inside.

It will take them less than ten minutes to steal every memory you have.

They can steal your memory, but they can't have your soul. For that is forever bound back in West Monroe.

Soon enough you will be back there, memories all in place, future stories left untold. For now.

## THE END

# TODAY

GOOD THING YOU PICKED BUCK. People forget about Buck Commander, your other business, but not you. You love it just as much as Duck Commander. And sure enough, choosing Buck takes you where you want to go.

It's good to be home. Back in a place where one of your children isn't missing. Back where Confederate generals aren't giving you the stink eye. Back where you belong.

After a big dinner and some family games, Korie opens her birthday presents. When she gets to yours, you prepare her, making sure she knows it's something very valuable *and* very meaningful. You can see her face light up.

That is, until she actually opens the present.

"It's a hat."

"A very special hat," you correct her.

"It's a Confederate soldier hat," she says, deadpan.

"Yes, but do you know who that belonged to?"

John Luke and Jase stare at you but don't say anything.

"I don't know," Korie says. "Robert E. Lee?"

"No! Stonewall Jackson. *The* Stonewall Jackson."

Korie nods. "That's great."

"Serious. That thing has to be worth some good money."

Korie puts on the hat.

"I think they sell those down at Walmart," Uncle Si says.

"No, no—it's real."

"It doesn't look real. Looks like it was made in Taiwan," Miss Kay says.

You shake your head. "No, it's real. I promise you."

"Thank you," Korie says, putting the hat back in the box.

"Look, it's real. I mean—it's as if I practically took it off Stonewall Jackson's head. Jase, doesn't it look real?"

He only shakes his head. "Nah, I don't think so."

You let out a sigh.

You travel through time and get a famous general's cap and still . . . nothing.

No respect.

Next time you go back in time, you'll borrow some jewels from some famous person. Because, as you know, women love the sparkly stuff.

## THE END

# TOMORROW

THE DOOR OF THE OUTHOUSE SHUTS with you inside.

Nothing happens.

You look above you, then around you. Then you decide to go ahead and take a seat.

You sit for a while. Waiting.

Trying to figure out where the others went.

You're sitting there in a wooden outhouse in your warehouse.

John Luke doesn't appear. Neither does Jase nor Uncle Si. You don't see or hear anything. But the more you sit on this round hole that's meant for other things, the more you find a certain sort of serenity. It's calm in here. It's so peaceful.

You think that maybe you should put this outhouse in your office, and then when people start to bother you, you can simply step inside and hide.

You don't wonder about the others for the moment, or whether it's Korie's birthday again, or even what you're going to have for lunch.

You sit in the outhouse and find contentment. It's a pretty rare thing these days.

Then a worry strikes you. There is peace and quiet in here, but in the end, what does it all mean?

## THE AMBIGUOUS ENDING

# 2319

YOU NEED TO GET OUT OF HERE NOW, so you press one of the screen images. It's a beach scene, so it can't be all that bad. Right?

You feel the vibration and the motion ramping up, so you hold on to a handle at the edge of a workstation until the movement stops. Then the door opens, yet the monitors don't say where you're at or what year it is.

"What'd you do?" Si asks.

"I saved us."

"You think it's safe to go out there?"

"I don't hear anybody," you say. "You think we're still invisible?"

You step closer to the door opening and hear the sound of the ocean.

*We're somewhere better. Somewhere we can get a tan.* But

you feel your bare head and face and know you won't be able to stay in the sun for too long.

"Ready?" you ask Si.

"Man, I was born ready. Born to be wild."

You shake your head. You're really not wanting anything wild. Not for a long time.

You step out of the machine but don't recognize your location. Your feet sink as you find yourself walking in soft sand. Then you see the water nearby.

"Hey, look—there's a horse," Si says.

He pulls the large beast toward you by its reins.

*Something doesn't feel right.*

Then again, you've just journeyed through time and space in an outhouse. Or in a time machine that looks like an outhouse, which might actually be worse. So lots of things don't feel right.

"I don't think this is West Monroe," Si says.

"Of course it's not West Monroe, Si! When was the last time you saw a beach in WM?"

You decide to hop on the horse, and Uncle Si gets up behind you. You don't see anything for miles. Just sand, with water on one side and forest on the other.

For a while the two of you ride in silence. No one is around. The sun is blinding. Sweat streams down your forehead and your back.

Then you stumble upon some massive building that blocks out the sun.

"What's that?" Si asks.

You stop the horse and dismount, staring up at the huge structure.

"I'm back. I'm home. All the time, it was . . . We finally really did it."

Then you recognize it. *No . . .*

You're standing in front of the Statue of Liberty, except half of her is buried in the sand.

You start to scream. "You maniacs! You blew it up! Nooooooooooo—"

## THE BEGINNING . . . OF THE END?

# TOMORROW

THE BIRTHDAY PARTY FOR KORIE was a huge success. She laughed at the picture of herself with John Luke, thinking you had done some fancy stuff with Photoshop. You ended up going outside later that night to check on the time machine, but it was gone, and John Luke and Si had no idea where it went.

Now it's lunchtime on the following day, and you head out of your office to find Jase. You're in the mood for a shrimp sandwich at Duck Diner. As you walk into the warehouse, you end up finding the wooden outhouse, looking just as it did the day before.

"No way." Someone's definitely playing a trick on you now.

You hear footsteps approaching—maybe it's the culprit. "Dad?"

You turn and see John Luke standing there. Wearing the same clothes as yesterday—same cap, same everything.

"Are we going?" he asks.

"Going where?"

"Going to get Mom's birthday present."

You look at him for a moment. *This isn't funny.* Then you keep looking at him.

"What?" John Luke asks.

"Come on."

"What?"

"Mom's birthday?"

He has no clue what you're getting at.

"Didn't we have the party *last* night?" you ask.

But once again, John Luke's face is blank. He changes the subject. "What is that?" he asks, pointing toward the outhouse. "Did you open it?"

*Okay, fine, I'll play along with Father Time.*

"*I'm* not opening that door," you say, repeating what you told him *yesterday.*

"Why not?"

"'Cause I think . . . I think maybe someone's playing a trick on me. Or I'm losing my mind. Which very well might be happening right now."

"I'll open it," John Luke says, grinning as he starts to tug on the handle.

"Hold on there," you say without any conviction.

John Luke opens it anyway.

"Maybe you shouldn't step inside that thing."

But he does. And soon the antennas are flashing. Just like yesterday, John Luke is missing when you open the door.

You remember what Si told you after he landed from parachuting.

*"There's been a space-time continuum problem. You have to go back to the future."*

It's either that or you'll probably be trapped inside this *Groundhog Day* forever and ever.

Living out the same day. Or days.

Day after day.

Week after week.

You get inside the machine. There's really no other option.

**Do you travel to the year 2319?**
**Go to page 71.**

**Do you just sit inside the machine without**
**doing anything? Go to page 225.**

# 2319

YOU'VE JUST THOUGHT of a way to persuade Si to come home when you hear something familiar. Now that the ship's engines are quiet, you can make out a song that sounds like the music from one of your favorite movies.

"Wow. That music—it's totally the way I'd imagine the future sounding," you tell Uncle Si.

"Oh, that? I downloaded the sound track to *Blade Runner*. For free. All art is free in the future. You can download music from artists before they release an album. Or watch a movie *while* they're making it. How cool is that?"

It sounds crazy to you.

"Look, Si, I've got some bad news for you."

"I'm already living in a world without sunlight—how can it be much worse?" he asks.

"I'm afraid I have to let you go from Duck Commander."

His mouth opens. "You can't do that, Jack!"

"Yes. It's been a hard decision to make."

"But you said you just got here," Si says.

"I know. That's why it's even more difficult."

"Well, I've never been fired from a job."

You shrug.

"I can't let that go on my record," Si continues.

"Yes. It would be tough to get future employment."

He nods. "If I go home with you, will you reinstate my job?"

"I'll think about it."

"Fair enough." He pauses for a moment, looking at the falling rain on the windshield of the aircraft. "So we're going to have to get to the time machine. It's in this building."

"Then let's go."

"The only thing is this: it's currently being guarded by almost a hundred men. They're all carrying automatic laser rifles, and they're also trained ninjas."

"That might be a problem," you say.

"We could enter the building with guns blazing. Like *Young Guns*. In a hail of glory."

"You're no young gun," you tell Si.

"Speak for yourself, Jack. I feel young."

"Are there any other options?" you ask.

"We can blow the place up and hope the time machine survives."

You shake your head. "Too risky."

"Look. We can dress up like them. They'll never know."

You know he'll be as blind as a bat if he takes off those glasses. But if he keeps them on, so much for your disguise.

"I have these bombs that stun men with smells. We could try that out on them. I think I have one that smells like pig guts."

You let out a laugh. "What will that do? Make the men sick to their stomachs?"

Si lets out a sigh. "I don't think we can get past them, then. It's impossible."

"There's nothing else we can do?" you ask.

"Well, we could make ourselves invisible."

You look to see if he's joking, and he's not. "Why didn't you say that in the first place?"

"Oh, that's so cliché. The whole invisible act."

"It'll work, though, right?"

Uncle Si nods.

"I like that a whole lot more than smelling pig guts."

• • •

It's a wild thing, being invisible. Walking so close to big, dangerous-looking men carrying guns and not even being glanced at. You and Uncle Si can see each other, but no one else is aware you're there. Si is leading you through various hallways, all lined with men standing guard and patrolling the area.

You arrive at a closed doorway that's guarded by a man with a large rifle. Si motions toward the door and gives a thumbs-up. You're not sure how you're going to get in without being noticed.

Si puts up a hand as if to say, *I got it*. Then he walks right over to the muscular guard. Without pause, he sticks his finger up the man's nose.

The guard jerks his head away and rubs his nose as if some bug flew up it. He's looking around for something, anything, but can't find what touched him.

When the guard finally stops messing with his nose, Si touches it again. Now the man starts slapping his face. Uncle Si is laughing silently.

Now Si sticks his finger in his own mouth.

"No," you whisper.

He just nods. Then he places the wet finger in the man's ear.

The guard loses it, pounding at his head and running down the hallway.

"That was easy," Si whispers.

You open the door and creep into the room, shutting the door behind you.

Sure enough, there's your outhouse, with the carving of the duck on the door and the antennas on the top. You never thought it would be such a welcome sight.

"Let's get inside," you say.

Someone knocks abruptly on the door to the room. Si looks over his shoulder.

"You get in," he says. "I can fight them off."

You press the button on the time machine door and pull on the handle to open it.

"Si, come on."

"Seriously. Only one of us will make it. Go ahead. Clearly the needs of the many outweigh the needs of the few."

You just stand there staring at him. "You're not *dying*, Si. You're not Spock. Come on; get in there."

Si gives you a long look before heading into the time machine. You follow him.

Once the door shuts, both you and Si get behind monitors, trying to figure out how to set the machine.

"How'd you get to the future, Uncle Si?"

"I was just pressing every button I could find."

Now you hear angry knocking on the time machine door.

"Is that locked?" you ask.

"I don't know!"

You pull up a screen full of about a hundred different images. None of them look familiar.

More pounding.

You guys have to leave this place.

You have to leave before they break open the door.

**Do you press one of the images on the screen?**
**Go to page 227.**

**Do you hope Si does something to save you both?**
**Go to page 169.**

**Do you wait and think of a better plan?**
**Go to page 51.**

# TODAY

JOHN LUKE DISAPPEARS when the door opens. He was right there, but suddenly . . . *boom*. He's gone.

Maybe it's some kind of weird time travel thing. Maybe he's back in your home. You don't know.

You step out, expecting to be inside the warehouse again. But instead you're in a small, square yard with a fence around it. You take a couple of strides and step in a big pile of poo. You glance around and see them everywhere. Wherever you look, you see more droppings. It's disgusting.

*Whoever lives here is a slob.*

The house behind you is a small one-story structure. There's a sliding-glass door leading to a small deck. You've never seen this place, so you don't know where you are.

You pull the phone out of your pocket but discover that

it's not yours. It's the old-school kind, a flip phone that can only call and text.

*Where'd my phone go?*

This is strange.

You knock on the glass door and see a face appear at the window. It's a face you recognize. Actually, one you just saw back at your prom revisit.

Yet this face is different too.

*Jill Baxter.*

Wow.

Just . . . wow.

But wait a minute. You know this can't be her because you saw her just a few months ago, before you ever discovered the time machine. She still acted all weird and creepy toward you, like she has since she started crushing on you in high school, but she didn't look like this. But there's no one else it could be.

"The door's open. Stop your knockin'," she says.

You turn the knob and enter a dim living room.

Jill is smoking a cigarette. Well, it's more like a cigarette is hanging from her lip in a way that says there's usually a cigarette hanging from her lip. You spot a tattoo of a bowling ball on her arm. She's wearing sweatpants and a T-shirt that says *Williebowl*.

For a second you stare at the image on the shirt because

the guy in the picture sorta looks like you. Except he's about two hundred pounds heavier.

"Uh, Jill?" you say.

She turns and meets your eyes. "You tryin' to be funny?"

"What?"

"Whatever." She heads into another room while you look around.

The place belongs in one of those shows about people who hoard things in their houses. The room is a disaster. There are boxes and clothes and bags of food and shoes and appliances and more boxes and garbage bags everywhere. Everywhere.

"Jill," you call after her, "I just need to explain why—"

"Why're you being so weird, Dad?"

A scrawny kid joins you in the living room. He's wearing really, really loose jeans—so loose they're basically down to his knees—and another Williebowl T-shirt. The boy kinda looks like you, but he also looks like . . . Jill.

*Oh no.*

"Hey—let me see that shirt."

It shows a bowling ball exploding into blood and guts.

"Where'd you get this?"

"You're funny. Aren't you supposed to be at work?"

You were going to explain about getting a birthday present for Korie, but then you realize something. Something terrible.

If this dippy-looking boy is your son, then you're not married to Korie. There's no John Luke or any of your other kids.

You must have made a mistake with the whole time travel thing. But what was it? What did you do wrong?

You start to feel a bit dizzy.

A gigantic dog smelling like onions comes up and licks your hand. You push him away, but not before he leaves thick spittle all over your fingers. You go to wipe it on your shirt, then notice what you're wearing.

It's a Williebowl shirt.

*No. This isn't happening.*

You also notice something else. You're a bit larger than you were before.

Like really, *really* out of shape.

You're wearing the same outfit Jill has on: a Williebowl shirt and a pair of sweatpants. Really tight sweatpants that don't feel good. The kind that give you a wedgie about ten minutes after you put them on.

You follow the kid (your son?) down the hall and trip over a bag of dog food. Actually, it's about four large bags of dog food. The boy ignores you and goes outside, letting the door slam behind him.

Then you see a picture hanging on the wall. It's Jill and you standing in front of a building with a sign that says . . .

Yep.

*Williebowl.*

You can't understand what happened.

Shouldn't you know since you're living this life now?

Isn't that how time travel works?

Something pops into your mind. *The note I left myself. About the Buffalo Bills.*

You make your way through the tiny house and find Jill back in the living room, smoking her cigarette and watching a housewives reality show.

"Jill—what, uh . . . ? Can I ask some silly questions?"

"Like what?" She doesn't even look at you.

*Friendly lady.*

"Did I ever . . . ? Do you know if I ever bet money on football?"

Her head snaps up and she gives you a mean look. "That's funny. What's gotten into you today?"

"I'm just wondering. Just tell me."

"Let's see—probably last week. Right? You don't tell me, but I know you do."

"Did I ever . . . ? Did I ever bet any on Super Bowls years ago?"

She stands and shakes her head. "When are you ever going to let it go? You made a lot of money. So what? We blew a lot of money. You and your *franchise*. You with all your branding ideas."

You look down at your T-shirt.

Williebowl.

"So wait a minute," you say. "I bet on the Buffalo Bills Super Bowls?"

Your "wife" laughs. "Yeah. The only bets you've ever made and won."

You go to rub your beard but find only a lip ring and a nose ring instead.

This can't be happening.

It was a simple, harmless note.

"Jill, I just—there's something wrong," you start to explain.

"Yeah, I'd say. Kingpin threw up all over the kitchen floor."

"Kingpin? That's our dog, right?"

She nods, then tosses you a ragged towel. Guess she wants you to clean it up.

You look outside to the backyard but can't find the outhouse. You've never wanted to see something more in your life.

So this is how it's going to be.

Williebowl and Kingpin.

Wonderful.

## THE END

# TODAY

YOU LEAVE JOHN LUKE OUTSIDE to see what's going on with Uncle Si. Considering who it is, you know that *anything* could be happening with him.

You have something else to do. And you have only a few moments to do it.

You end up managing to sneak inside without Korie seeing you. Then you get to work.

• • •

Korie's birthday dinner is a big family event. Phil and Miss Kay are here. So's Uncle Si. Jase, Jep, Alan, and their wives and kids—everybody is here.

Several times during the meal, you look at John Luke and smile. Neither of you say anything since . . . Well, what would you say? *"Yeah, John Luke and I went back to 1990 this afternoon. It was a blast."*

No.

For now, it'll be a secret. Maybe you can show Korie the time machine later.

After dinner, everybody gathers in the family room to watch Korie open presents. Even though she's said she doesn't want or need anything, people still brought her something.

As she opens her gifts, you tell her to choose yours last.

"This is from Willie and John Luke," Korie finally announces. "Who forgot to get something?" she asks, smiling at the fact that this is a combined gift. The other kids have managed to get Mom a present on their own.

"This is a special gift that *both* of us worked on," you say.

She opens it up and examines the framed picture within. Her grin reveals that she loves it.

"This is great!" she says. "It looks so real too."

"Let me see," Uncle Si says.

Korie shows off the picture of John Luke with his arm around her. The only thing is, she's eighteen years old and dressed for prom.

"I didn't know you guys were this good

at Photoshop," Korie says. "And look at John Luke. I bet I would've gotten the two of you confused back in high school. Especially with that mullet."

John Luke raises his eyebrows at you.

The gift is perfect.

• • •

Later on, after everybody has gone home, John Luke comes in from the backyard.

"Hey, Dad," he says in a whisper. "The outhouse—time machine—whatever you want to call it . . ."

"Yeah?"

"It's gone."

"Really? Are you sure?"

"Yeah. I looked around everywhere for it."

And you were really hoping you could show Korie the machine.

"Oh, well. That was fun while it lasted."

"One other thing," John Luke says with worry all over his face.

"What is it?"

"I can't find Sadie. Anywhere. It's like she just . . . disappeared."

## THE END . . . OR IS IT?

# THE MORNING FOG
## A Note from John Luke Robertson

I LOVE THE IDEA of traveling in time. Being able to go back in time to meet someone like Jesus and see some of his miracles would be incredible. I also love the idea of going back in time to make up for dumb things I've done.

This past February would be one of those times I'd set the redneck time machine for.

It was a day after we'd gotten some snow and rain. The fields were muddy and perfect for driving around on and doing donuts. My Jeep is great for those sorts of things. So I was out driving around doing donuts when suddenly—*boom!* A tree came out of nowhere.

Actually, the tree had always been there. I just totally didn't see it. It seemed to appear out of thin air, and my Jeep crashed right into it.

Our lives are like that. It's so easy to be doing the right thing at the right time, and then, out of nowhere, a tree comes and we crash. It can be something we say or do. It can be anything. We're all prone to making mistakes.

The great thing is that God doesn't keep us stranded back in time because of our mistakes. That's the beauty of grace. Mistakes can sure change our lives, sometimes for the worse. But God never gives up on us. Like a father, he continues to watch over us and love us and wants us to make the right decisions.

It's so easy to look ahead to next week or next month or even next year or to look back and wish things had been different. The last few years, being part of the Robertson family has been quite a wild adventure. Sometimes it's easy to try to look too far into the future. But God's Word is a reminder to stay focused on today.

James 4:14 says, "How do you know what your life will be like tomorrow? Your life is like the morning fog—it's here a little while, then it's gone."

Even if I live to be one hundred years old, my life will still be like the morning fog. Hovering around, then suddenly gone.

My hope is that I can continue the Robertson legacy and shine a light on our faith and values. To make some sense of the morning fog. Just for a moment, maybe.

That's my hope for you too.

# FOR MORE FUN & WACKY ADVENTURES READ ALL FOUR BOOKS!

## WILLIE'S REDNECK TIME MACHINE

Willie and John Luke stumble through time.

## PHIL & THE GHOST OF CAMP CH-YO-CA

John Luke and Phil check out some strange happenings at a summer camp.

## SI IN SPACE

Si and John Luke get stuck In an out-of-this-world adventure.

## JASE & THE DEADLIEST HUNT

John Luke, Jase, and the crew are invited to participate in the hunt of their lives.